Brotherly Love

Christy® Fiction Series

Christy® Fiction Series

Brotherly Love

Catherine Marshall
adapted by C. Archer

Thomas Nelson, Inc.

Nashville

BROTHERLY LOVE
Book Twelve in the *Christy*® Fiction Series

Copyright © 1997
by the Estate of Marshall-LeSourd L.L.C.

The *Christy*® Fiction Series is based on *Christy*®
by Catherine Marshall LeSourd © 1967
by Catherine Marshall LeSourd

The *Christy*® name and logo are officially registered
trademarks of the Estate of Marshall-LeSourd L.L.C.

Managing Editor: Laura Minchew
Project Editor: Beverly Phillips

Library of Congress Cataloging-in-Publication Data

Archer, C. 1956–
    Brotherly love / Catherine Marshall ; adapted by C. Archer.
        p.   cm. — (Christy fiction series ; 12)
    Summary: When Christy's charming fifteen-year-old brother
turns up at the mission with tales of a fire at his boarding school,
Christy feels that he is not telling the truth, and sets out to
discover the real story.
    ISBN 0-8499-3963-1
    [1. Brothers and Sisters—Fiction 2. Teachers—Fiction
3. Honesty—Fiction. 4. Conduct of life—Fiction 5. Christian
life—Fiction.] I. Marshall, Catherine, 1914–1983. Christy.
II. Title. III. Series : Archer, C., 1956– Christy fiction series; 12.
    PZ7.A6744Bt   1997
    [Fic]—dc21   97–11071
                                                                              CIP
                                                                               AC

Printed in the United States of America

97 98 99 00 OPM 9 8 7 6 5 4 3 2 1

The Characters

CHRISTY RUDD HUDDLESTON, a nineteen-year-old schoolteacher in Cutter Gap.

GEORGE HUDDLESTON, Christy's fifteen-year-old brother.

MR. AND MRS. HUDDLESTON, Christy's parents.

AUNT LUCY, Christy's aunt.

GRANDMOTHER AND GRANDFATHER HUDDLESTON, Christy's grandparents.

CHRISTY'S STUDENTS:
CREED ALLEN, age nine.
LITTLE BURL ALLEN, age six.
BESSIE COBURN, age twelve.
RUBY MAE MORRISON, age thirteen.
MOUNTIE O'TEALE, age ten.
CLARA SPENCER, age twelve.
JOHN WASHINGTON, age ten.

PRINCE, a black stallion.

GOLDIE, Miss Alice's palomino mare.

DAVID GRANTLAND, the young minister.

IDA GRANTLAND, David's sister and the mission housekeeper.

ALICE HENDERSON, a Quaker missionary from Ardmore, Pennsylvania, who helped start the mission at Cutter Gap.

RICHARD BENTON, George's roommate at school.

ABIGAIL BENTON, Richard's little sister.

DR. NEIL MACNEILL, the physician of the Cove.

BEN PENTLAND, the mailman.

MR. KOLLER, headmaster at the Bristol Academy.

GRANNY O'TEALE, an elderly superstitious mountain woman.

JACK O'DELL, acquaintance of Dr. MacNeill's.

MR. DRAKE, George's English teacher.

FAIRLIGHT SPENCER, a mountain woman who is a good friend of Christy's.

MR. BURNS, George's Latin teacher.

MISS MURKOFF, Mr. Koller's secretary.

PETER SMITHERS, a student at the Bristol Academy.

✌ One ✌

Miz Christy, I brung you some flowers. Some *magic* flowers."

Christy Huddleston smiled at nine-year-old Creed Allen, one of her most mischievous students. He stood before her desk, smiling his Tom Sawyer grin. His hands were empty.

"Invisible flowers," she exclaimed. "My favorite kind!" She made a show of accepting her imaginary bouquet. "Thank you, Creed. Now it's time to get to your seat. The noon break is over, and we've got an English lesson waiting."

"They ain't invisible, Miz Christy," Creed insisted. "They's *magic*."

He glanced over his shoulder at his classmates, who were watching him expectantly. Then, with a flourish, he waved his hand.

Suddenly, to Christy's amazement, he presented her with a bouquet of brightly colored paper flowers.

1

"Creed!" she cried. "They're beautiful! But . . . how did you ever—"

"Like I said," Creed said, strutting back to his desk, "they's magic."

Christy examined the colorful "bouquet." It was a simple magic trick. In fact, her own brother, George, used to perform the same trick when he was younger. But where on earth would a poor child like Creed get hold of something like this? Her students' families couldn't afford shoes or food, let alone magic paper flowers!

"You know, my little brother used to do a magic trick like this," Christy said.

"You mean George?" Creed asked.

"Why, yes. I guess I must have mentioned him before."

"No'm."

"Then how did you know his name?"

Creed grinned from ear to ear. "Could be 'cause he's hidin' behind that there blackboard, a-waitin' to surprise you!"

Before Christy could utter another word, out jumped George from behind the blackboard. He ran to her, lifted her right up out of her chair, and swung her around in a circle.

"Hey, there, Sis! Surprised?"

"George! I can't believe it's really you!" Christy laughed. "Now, please put me down. I'm getting dizzy."

George looked like their father, with his chiseled chin and his deep blue eyes framed by dark lashes. However, their faither had a solemn, worried air about him, but George always seemed ready to take on the world. And, like their mother, he had an infectious laugh and a dimpled grin that was hard to ignore.

Christy had also inherited their father's blue eyes, but she had their mother's delicate build. And when it came to personality, she was much more like their father than George was. She was responsible, kind, and quick to worry.

"Class," Christy said, straightening her dress, "I'd like you to meet my brother, George Huddleston."

"Oh, I've already met a few of these characters," George said, winking at Creed. "I taught Creed that magic trick during the break while you were reading to some of the other children. He's a quick study."

"How long have you been here?"

"Oh, just an hour or so. I walked from El Pano. Got lost a few hundred times. Then I did a quick tour of the mission. Love what you've done with the place, by the way."

"I don't understand," Christy said. "Shouldn't you be at boarding school?"

George rolled his eyes. "So much for the postal service. Didn't you get my letter?"

"Letter? No. I haven't had a letter from you in ages, George," Christy shook a finger at him, "even though I write you every single week."

"I know, I know—I'm the world's lousiest correspondent. But they keep us pretty busy at school, Sis. The thing is, I *did* write to tell you I was coming," he grinned, "Or warn you, I guess I should say."

"Don't be silly." Christy gave him a hug. "You know I'm thrilled to see you. But what about school?"

George picked up a piece of chalk from the blackboard. "We had a big storm the other day. It caused a lot of damage. The place is going to be closed for a couple of weeks while they do repairs."

"That's a shame."

"Well, it depends on your point of view. Most of us were pretty excited."

"Is it my turn?" Bessie asked as she gazed at George.

"Yes," said George rather matter-of-factly. "Introducing Bessie."

Bessie twirled in a circle and began pulling handkerchief's from George's coat sleeve. To the group's amusement, George acted more astonished with each handkerchief's appearance. As the laughter died down, George ran to the blackboard.

With a few quick strokes, George drew a

picture of Christy on the blackboard. In it, she was holding a paper flower in her teeth while she graded a stack of papers that towered to the ceiling.

The children laughed uproariously. Christy had to admit it was a very funny portrait. George had always been an excellent artist. In fact, he was good at almost anything he tried—when he applied himself.

"All right, class, settle down," Christy said, smiling in spite of her stern tone. "My brother is allowed to draw funny pictures of me, but I don't want the rest of you getting any ideas!"

"Well, well. Don't you sound just like a real teacher!" George exclaimed.

"I *am* a real teacher," Christy replied, trying not to sound defensive. She grabbed the eraser and removed the picture while the children groaned. "You know, I don't remember hearing anything about a bad storm around those parts," she said. "You'd think Mother might have mentioned it. I just got a letter from her yesterday."

George didn't answer. He turned to the class and said, "How about one more magic trick for the road?"

They applauded wildly. Christy sat at her desk and watched her crazy, wonderful, unpredictable brother "pull" a coin out of Mountie O'Teale's right ear.

Christy shook her head. Clearly, she had her work cut out for her. It was going to be very hard to top *that* performance with another grammar lesson.

❧ TWO ❧

"My, my, will you look at that boy eat?" exclaimed Miss Ida at dinner that evening.

George ladled out another huge helping of mashed potatoes. "Finest food I've eaten in a long time, Miss Ida. You're the real magician around here."

Miss Ida smiled. "Your brother is such a charmer," she said to Christy.

Christy grinned with pride. Only a few hours had passed since George's arrival, and already everyone at the mission seemed to like her brother.

Miss Alice, who'd helped found the mission, had told Christy how bright and entertaining she found George. David Grantland, the mission's young minister, laughed uproariously at George's jokes. Miss Ida, David's sister, was clearly charmed.

And as for Ruby Mae Morrison, the thirteen-year-old girl who lived at the mission house—well, she was absolutely smitten. Christy could tell. She'd seen Ruby Mae and her friends go through all kinds of crushes at school. And if the doe-eyed look Ruby Mae was directing at George was any indication, Ruby Mae was already head-over-heels in love.

"Miss Ida, I ate up all your chicken, too," Ruby Mae said, grabbing for the last of the mashed potatoes. "How come you never compliment *my* eatin'?"

"Because you eat more than five full-grown men put together," Miss Ida scolded.

"Nonsense," Christy said, winking at Ruby Mae. "Ruby Mae has a normal, healthy appetite. Just like me."

George laughed. "It's true. Christy could out-eat me any day of the week." He shook his head. "I still cannot believe my big sister is a real, live teacher. To me, she's still just a kid with pigtails and dirty knees, playing with spiders."

"Spiders!" Miss Ida exclaimed.

"Oh, Christy always loved to learn about insects. It used to drive Mother crazy." George shrugged. "She always liked to find out where and how they live."

"So you're attending the Bristol Academy this year?" David asked. "Is that anywhere near Asheville?"

George finished off his glass of milk. "It's in Cullowhee, not too far from there."

"How do you like the school?" asked Miss Alice.

"I like it fine, although it's hard work, and the teachers are tough graders."

"Just like Miz Christy," Ruby Mae said softly. "I'll bet you're the smartest boy there, George."

"Hardly!" George scoffed.

"George doesn't always apply himself, Ruby Mae," Christy said, smiling at her brother. "If he did, there's no telling what he could accomplish."

"I don't always apply myself, neither," Ruby Mae admitted to George. "Applyin' makes my head spin."

"Ruby Mae, I think you and I are going to get along just fine," George said.

Ruby Mae gazed back at George like a lovesick puppy.

"So how long will you be able to stay, George?" David asked.

"A couple of weeks, at least. Maybe even longer. The fire did a lot of damage. Who knows?" George grinned at Christy. "Maybe I'll just stay here forever."

"Wait a minute," Christy said, frowning. "I—"

"All right, all right." George held up his hands. "I promise I won't stay forever, Sis."

"No, that's not what I meant. Did you just say *fire*? I thought you said the school was damaged by a big storm."

George paused to butter a roll before replying. "It was. But a fire started when one of the dormitory buildings was hit by lightning. That's where most of the damage was. Unfortunately, that's also where I was housed."

"What's your roommate doing while the repairs are being done?" Christy asked.

"Richard? I . . . I'm not sure. I think he decided to go home to Richmond. You know how he is. Very unpredictable."

"Well, all I know about him is what you mentioned in your letters. Which, I might add again, are far too infrequent. I hope you write Mother and Father more often."

"Not much," George admitted sheepishly. "Which reminds me . . . I didn't exactly tell them about my coming here."

"Why not?"

"You know how Mother is. I was afraid she'd be upset if she knew I was visiting you instead of going home." George met Christy's eyes. "So maybe we should keep this visit under our hats, if you know what I mean."

"Oh, I'm sure she'll understand, George. It's been ages since you and I have seen each other."

"Still," George said, a little more forcefully, "let's just keep it between you and me."

Christy hesitated. It didn't seem right, not mentioning something this exciting to her parents. She always told them everything in her letters.

"It's not like you'd be lying, Sis. We'd just be omitting a little information to spare someone's feelings." George turned to David. "What do you think, Reverend? You're an expert on such things."

"No, no." David shoved back his chair. "I'm off duty, George. And I don't want to get in the middle of a family dispute."

"I have an idea." George snapped his fingers. "I'll stop by Mother and Father's for a few days before it's time to go back to school. It'll be a complete surprise. In the meantime, not a word to them, Christy."

"All right. I hate to have you leave even a few days early, but Mother and Father will be thrilled to see you."

George gathered up some glasses and silverware. "I'll take care of the dishes tonight, Miss Ida. You've done enough." He motioned to Ruby Mae. "Come on, Ruby Mae. Give me a hand, and I'll tell you all about what Christy was like as a little girl. Did you know she sucked her thumb till she was ten?"

"Go on!" Ruby Mae cried.

"George Huddleston," Christy chided. "Don't you start—"

"All right, all right." George paused at the kitchen door. "I'm exaggerating slightly. But she did sleep with her stuffed bear, Mr. Buttons, right up until she left for Cutter Gap."

Miss Alice chuckled. "He's wonderful, Christy."

"An angel," Miss Ida said, "an absolute angel."

Christy laughed. "Well, I'm not sure I'd go that far."

She watched as George and Ruby Mae headed into the kitchen. George might not be an angel, but he was a wonderful brother. It would be great to have him here for a while to catch up on old times.

Christy found herself stopping to think about George's behavior. Why did she have this uneasy feeling that there was something not quite right about this visit?

❧ Three ❧

Slowly, carefully, George unpacked his belongings. He almost wondered if he should bother. It wasn't like he'd be staying here long.

He sat on the edge of his bed. It was covered by a threadbare but clean quilt. A battered wooden dresser, a chair, and a washstand completed the furnishings in the simple room. Not for the first time, George wondered about his sister's choice to work at the mission.

How different this was from the home they'd grown up in! The Huddlestons weren't a rich family. But compared to this spare house, their home back in Asheville practically looked like a palace.

George unpacked his socks and hairbrush. Then he reached to the bottom of his suitcase and pulled out a framed photograph.

The picture had been taken when George was eight years old. In it, George, Christy, and their parents were posed together formally. Mr. Huddleston looked stiff and dour. Mrs. Huddleston was smiling radiantly. George, as usual, was mugging for the camera.

But it was Christy's smile that made George love this photo so much. She wasn't looking at the camera. Instead, she was looking at George with a patient, loving, big-sister smile. It seemed to say, "I'll always take care of you, even if you *are* a lot of trouble, little brother."

He was startled by a gentle knock on his door. "George? It's Christy. May I come in?"

"Sure."

Christy stepped inside. "I just wanted to see if there's anything else you need."

"Nope. I'm all set." George spread his arms wide. "All the comforts of home."

Christy gave a wry smile. "This probably makes your dormitory look like a fancy hotel."

"I've got a bed. That's all I really need." George closed his suitcase and set it aside. "Although I have to admit that I'm impressed you've stayed here this long, Christy. How long have you been teaching at the mission now?"

"Almost a year."

George whistled. "To tell you the truth, I

probably would've hightailed it out of here the first day. I don't think I could stand the hardship."

"Actually, the mission is luxurious."

"Luxurious?" George cried.

"Yes, compared to most of the cabins around here." Christy went to the window and sighed. "These beautiful mountains! You'd never believe they could hide such poverty, George. Most of my students have never even owned a pair of shoes."

"It must be hard."

"Yes. And yet they're so brave and full of joy."

George shook his head. "I meant hard for *you*. This isn't your life, Christy."

"It is now."

"I mean, this isn't the way you were raised. And some people might say this isn't even your problem."

"But it is." Christy smiled that sweet, reassuring smile of hers. "I *chose* to be here. And I'm glad I did." She laughed. "Don't get me wrong. I mean, I had plenty of doubts at first. I almost gave up more than once. But I'm so glad I had the strength, with God's help, to stay. These people have given me so much more than I've given them."

For a moment, George just stared at his sister. They'd grown up together. They had spent every Christmas and Easter and Fourth of July together. They had enjoyed long, lazy summer vacations together.

And yet, looking at her now, she seemed like a stranger. Not only did she look different—older, stronger, more mature—she *seemed* different.

"How did you know, Sis?" George asked softly. "How did you know you made the right choice coming here?"

"I gave it time. I listened to my heart. And I prayed." Christy paused. "Then one day I looked out the window at those beautiful mountains, and I just knew this was the place I belonged, and this was the work I was meant to do."

George placed his belongings in the top drawer of his dresser. "I wonder if I'll ever feel that way. I never seem to know what the right thing to do is."

"You're only fifteen, George. You're not supposed to have all the answers."

"Oh, and you have all the answers at nineteen?"

Christy laughed. "Hardly." She reached for George's photo and grinned. "I remember when we had this picture taken. You refused to sit still. And you kept making an awful face at the poor photographer."

"That was just my natural expression."

"I'm so glad you're here. I've missed you. You know what I was thinking about the other day? Remember how we used to go to the church conference at Montreat every summer?"

"I think that's where your fascination with bugs really started."

"Well, I may have loved insects, but I certainly hated the water. You, on the other hand, were part fish from the day you were born." Christy sat on the edge of George's bed. "Anyway, I remember the day you tried to coax me into jumping off the pier into the lake. I kept saying I knew I would drown. And you kept promising you'd catch me." She sighed. "Finally, I jumped in. That had to be the hardest leap of faith I've ever made in my life. Harder even than coming here to work at the mission."

George squeezed her hand. "I'll always be there to catch you, Sis." He grinned. "Although, to be fair, you do weigh a whole lot more now than you did back then."

Christy swatted his arm playfully, then headed to the door. "If there's anything you need, just yell."

George watched the door close. He sighed. He needed Christy's help right now, and yet he could not bring himself to ask for her help. Could he trust Christy to stand by him now, or was that asking too much? George had a secret that he could not bear to share—not even with his big sister.

George's secret required more courage

than he could muster up, at least for now. That was a leap of faith that would have to wait for another day.

❧ Four ❧

Aﾠnd then there was the time she drew freckles on her face with a pencil. Seems she thought they'd make her look more sophisticated!"

Christy put her hands on her hips and groaned. They were talking about her again! George and Doctor MacNeill had been sitting on the mission house porch for the last hour, chatting and laughing. Three days had passed since George's arrival. It seemed as if there was no one in Cutter Gap he hadn't charmed by now. "George," she chided, "are you telling more stories about me?"

"Oh, I've learned all kinds of fascinating things about your childhood, Christy." Doctor MacNeill took a puff on his pipe. "For example, I found it fascinating to discover that before you decided to become a teacher, you aspired to be a beekeeper."

"That lasted about a week," Christy said as she sat down next to George. She shot her brother her most withering glance, but he just grinned good-naturedly. "You know, I could be telling all kinds of stories about your childhood, too."

"We haven't just been talking about you," Doctor MacNeill said. "Your brother's been keeping me in stitches. He has quite a repertory of jokes. Why, I'd say he's ready for the stage."

"You two really seem to be enjoying each other's company," Christy said.

"The doctor invited me over for dinner," George said. "He tells me he's quite the cook."

"I wouldn't know," Christy said, with just a hint of resentment. "I haven't had the chance to sample much of Neil's cooking."

"That's not true!" Doctor MacNeill exclaimed. "How about that picnic I took you on? I made corn on the cob and ham biscuits."

"Yes, but it took you months to invite me. You've only known George an hour."

The doctor's dark eyes sparkled. "Well, you don't know magic tricks, Christy," he teased. "George does."

George stood and stretched. It still amazed Christy to see how much taller he'd grown since she had last seen him. He was practically a man now—though she still couldn't help feeling he was her "little" brother.

"Well," he said, "I think I'll take a walk down to David's bunkhouse. He said he could use some help rebuilding his fireplace. Besides—" he winked at Doctor MacNeill, "I'm sure you two would like some time alone."

"What have you been telling him?" Christy asked as George headed off.

"Nothing but the truth. He asked if we were involved."

"And you said . . ."

"I said I wasn't sure," the doctor squeezed Christy's hand, "but that I hoped so."

Christy felt a blush creep into her cheeks. "And what did George say to that?"

"He said he thought the reverend seemed interested in you, too. I told George he was an astute observer." The doctor paused to tamp down the tobacco in his pipe. "Then he said he thought David was a great fellow."

"And you said . . ."

"I said he wasn't as astute an observer as I'd thought."

"Neil!"

The doctor chuckled. "I'm just pulling your leg. You ought to be used to that, growing up with George."

"True enough."

"He's great, Christy. You're a lucky girl to have him for a brother."

"Well, not altogether lucky," Christy said,

staring off at the garden to avoid the doctor's gaze.

"Meaning what?"

"It's just that he's been a bit of a disrupting influence at school. He asked if he could sit in on my class for a while, and of course I said yes. But before I knew it, he was disrupting everything. He had half the students trying to pull things out of their neighbors' ears."

"Excuse me?"

"You know the old trick, where you pull a penny out from behind someone's ear? Well, George taught the children the trick during the noon recess yesterday, and of course, pandemonium broke loose. Creed pulled an acorn out of Little Burl's ear. Ruby Mae pulled a hair ribbon out of Bessie's ear. Wraight even pulled a field mouse out of Lundy's ear."

The doctor pretended to look worried. "Remind me to check the children's hearing next time I'm here."

"I know it sounds funny, Neil. But the children are so in love with George that they barely pay any attention to me anymore. He's like the Pied Piper."

"It's just the novelty of a new face, Christy. Besides, he's only going to be here a couple of weeks at the most. It's silly to get jealous."

"I'm not jealous!" Christy cried, but as soon as the words were out of her mouth, she realized they weren't true. "Well, maybe I'm a little jealous." She sighed. "The truth is, I suppose I've always been a little bit jealous of George. Everyone always falls in love with him instantly. It takes me longer to get to know people. I'm shy. I don't tell jokes well. I can never remember the punch lines. And George is so . . ." Christy threw up her hands. "I don't know. So easy to like."

The doctor leaned over and planted a soft kiss on her cheek. "You're pretty easy to like yourself."

"Thanks, Neil, but you're biased."

"Actually, I would think you'd be a tough act for George to follow. You were the first child. You always excelled in school. And now you're here, doing something brave and difficult."

"Hmm. I never thought of it that way."

"I got the impression that George really looks up to you, Christy."

"Did he . . ." Christy hesitated, "did he happen to say anything else?"

"About what?"

"Oh, I don't know," Christy said casually. "About school. Any troubles he might be having."

"No, not a thing. Why?"

She shrugged her shoulders. "Just a feeling. I can't really explain it. I just have a hunch George isn't telling me the whole truth about why he's here."

"The storm—"

"Yes, I know. Like I said, it's just a hunch. Call it woman's intuition."

"Maybe," the doctor said, "you're looking for a problem where none exists because you're feeling a little uncomfortable about having George here."

Christy shook her head. "It could be you're right. I'll think about it. In any case, that's quite enough about my problems for one day. How about we try tackling yours for a while?"

"Mine?"

"For instance, what do you plan to feed George and me for dinner when we visit?"

"I don't recall inviting you," the doctor said with a sly smile.

"But you were going to."

"And how can you be so sure of that?"

"It's just a hunch. Call it woman's intuition."

Five

Sit next to me this afternoon, George!"

"No, me!"

"No, *me*!"

Christy ran to the rescue and pulled George out of the knot of girls surrounding him. As was usual during the noon recess, he had been the center of attention.

"My brother and I need to talk, girls," Christy said. Her words were met with a chorus of groans.

"Thanks for the rescue," George said, wrapping his arm around Christy's shoulder as they strode toward the schoolhouse steps.

"Normally, the boys and girls don't even like to sit near each other," Christy pointed out. "Do you realize that half the girls in my class are madly in love with you?"

"Only half?" George joked.

"Seriously. You'd better watch your step,

or you'll have Ruby Mae and Bessie battling over you."

"Like the reverend and the doctor are battling over you?" George wiggled his eyebrows in a teasing way. "Shouldn't they be dueling at dawn any day now?"

"They've called a truce," Christy grinned, "at least temporarily."

Christy and George paused on the schoolhouse steps. Out on the lawn, the children were gathered in small groups, waiting for the afternoon classes to begin.

"Mother said the reverend asked you to marry him," George said.

"He did. But I wasn't ready for a commitment like that. And I have . . . feelings for Neil."

"I thought so. Well, if you want my two cents' worth, either one would make a fine brother-in-law."

"I'll keep that in mind."

"And in the meantime, if Ruby Mae and Bessie inquire about *my* availability," George said, "just tell them I'm not ready for a commitment like that, either."

Christy went to ring the bell that signaled the end of the break, but just then, she remembered something. "I almost forgot. Miss Alice gave me a letter this morning. Mr. Pentland, the mailman, delivered it to her cabin by mistake. It's for you." Christy reached into the pocket of her long skirt and passed the envelope to George.

He glanced at the envelope, scowled, and stuffed it into his own pocket.

"It's from Richard, isn't it?" Christy asked. "I'd have thought you'd be glad to hear from him."

"Naw," George shrugged, "now he'll expect a response. You know what a lousy letter-writer I am."

"I noticed that the return address was from your school," Christy said, "but I thought you said Richard was going home to Richmond while they did repairs. I mean, the dormitory can't be lived in, right?"

"Hey, I don't go around reading *your* mail, do I?" George snapped.

"I'm sorry. You're right. It's just that I happened to notice the return address."

Instantly, George's expression softened. "I'm sorry, Sis. I didn't mean to bite your head off. Richard probably sent the letter from the train station before he left for Richmond. That's why he used the school's address."

"Oh, of course. That makes sense."

"So, time to ring the bell?" George asked.

"Ring away."

While George rang for the children, Creed Allen and John Washington dashed over to Christy. "Miz Christy?" Creed asked. "Is we a-havin' story time today?"

"Yes, Creed," Christy nodded. "I wouldn't miss it for the world."

She loved telling the children stories as

much as she knew they loved hearing them. Since the school was too poor to afford books, sometimes Christy told Bible stories. Sometimes she recounted Aesop's fables, or stories she remembered reading as a child. And sometimes she just made up tales out of her own head. "As a matter of fact," Christy said, "I have a wonderful story in mind—"

"We was wonderin' somethin', Teacher," John interrupted, "that is, if'n you don't mind. We was wonderin' if maybe George could do the storytellin' today."

Christy hesitated. "George?"

"He's a powerful fine storyteller, Teacher," Creed said excitedly. "Keeps you in stitches, he does."

"Well, I suppose," Christy said slowly, "if George wants to tell you a story, it would be all right."

"Hooray!" John cried.

Christy watched as the two boys sprinted inside. She'd never seen them so excited about story time. At this rate, George would be ready to replace her before the week was out.

She wondered if anybody would even notice she was gone.

~ ~ ~

After school, George walked down to the little pond near the mission house. It took a while to lose his trail of fans—Ruby Mae, Bessie, and Clara. But finally he found a quiet spot where he could be alone.

George took out the letter from Richard and opened it. The pages shook in his trembling hand.

He was not going to read the note. What was the point? There was nothing Richard could say to change what had happened.

There was nothing anyone could say.

Another letter would be coming soon enough. George could imagine his mother's beautiful handwriting. He could almost read her impassioned words. He could almost see the blurred ink, stained by tears.

As soon as she found out what had happened, she would write Christy. It shouldn't be much longer. He'd have to be ready to leave by then.

Slowly, George crumpled the letter into a tight ball. He tossed it far, far out into the pond. It took a few moments to sink, but when it finally disappeared beneath the calm gray-blue water, he felt relieved.

That part of George's life was over. He was never going back to school. He was never going home again.

As George pondered his situation, only one question remained: where *was* he going from here?

⨳ Six ⨳

That evening, Christy crawled into bed with her diary. She'd gone to bed early. George was still downstairs with Miss Ida, Miss Alice, and David. From time to time, their laughter drifted up the stairs. Each time she heard their voices, Christy cringed a little.

She got out her pen and thumbed through the well-worn pages of her diary. Soon she would need to get another one. This one was nearly full. Full of the daily events of her life here at the mission. Full of hopes and fears and tears and laughter.

She was proud of this diary and what it represented. It was the story of her biggest triumph—coming here to teach. It was about learning, and growing, and making dear friends.

Her life in Cutter Gap was precious to her. It was an adventure of her own choosing. Hers, and hers alone.

Was that why she was feeling resentful about George's presence here? Did she feel as if this were her territory—something she didn't want to share, not even with her own brother?

Christy opened her diary to a fresh page. After a moment, she began to write:

I suppose I need to accept that Neil was right—I am jealous of George. As embarrassed as I am to admit that, it's the truth.

I love my brother dearly. But around him, I always feel like the little *sister. People are drawn to him. Even my students seem to prefer him to me.*

I know I shouldn't feel this way. But when I was sitting there at school today, listening to the children giggle at George's silly version of "Jack and the Beanstalk," I felt the old green-eyed monster—jealousy—eating away at me, the same way it did when I was a little girl and George sometimes stole away my parents' attention.

On top of all this, I still have lingering doubts about the real reason George is here. Today, for example, he acted oddly when I asked him about a letter he'd received.

Maybe I'm imagining things. Could it be that Neil is right, and I'm just looking for problems that aren't there because I'm feeling resentful of George?

Neil invited George and me to dinner tomorrow night. I have to admit that for a moment, even that simple, kind gesture from Neil made me resent George.

Just then, the sound of loud laughter met Christy's ears. She sighed and set down her pen.

A phrase from the Bible flashed into her head: "Charity envieth not."

Yes, the doctor had been right. It was jealousy she was feeling, all right.

She certainly hoped there was a cure.

— — —

"And if'n I add four and eight, then I got me thirteen?" Creed asked Christy the next day.

"Close, Creed." Christy took a deep breath.

It was time for arithmetic lessons, and as usual, the children were struggling. Why was she having such a hard time teaching addition to these children?

She'd asked David, who helped with the arithmetic classes, for advice, but he'd just smiled and counseled, "Patience, Christy. That's the secret. You need a sense of humor, and the patience of Job."

But with seventy children to teach and virtually no supplies, sometimes patience was hard to come by. Christy gazed around the room. The children were laboring over their chalkboards, doing the addition problems she'd assigned—harder tasks for the older students, simple counting for the very youngest.

"Try again, Creed," Christy urged.

The boy looked dejected. "I could figger it, I reckon, if'n I just had more fingers."

George, who was sitting nearby, signaled Christy. "Why don't I give a whack at explaining things?"

Christy's first reaction was to be annoyed. After all, *she* was the one with the teaching experience. *She* was the one who'd studied to become a teacher. George was just a high school student—and, come to think of it, not exactly a genius at mathematics, either.

On the other hand, she had sixty-nine other students in need of her attention.

"All right," Christy agreed. "Creed, George is going to explain this addition problem to you. Is that all right with you?"

"Sure thing," Creed said excitedly, clearly relieved to be exchanging instructors.

"Just don't do the work for him," Christy cautioned.

George gave her a mock salute. "Aye aye, Captain."

For the next few minutes, Christy made her way around the classroom, correcting students and answering questions. In the corner, George and Creed were giggling away. It hardly sounded like George was teaching the boy anything.

Just then, Ben Pentland, the mailman, appeared in the doorway. "Howdy, Miz

Christy," he said. "I got a letter for you. Been a busy week for mail at the mission. Looks like this one's from Asheville."

George looked over. "From Mother?" he called.

"Probably," Christy replied, "I'm about due for another one."

"You sure it's not for me?" George asked, sounding oddly strained.

"Nope. Says to 'Miss Christy Huddleston,' plain as day," Mr. Pentland said.

"Don't worry, George. I'll let you read it," Christy said. She shook her head. "You know, you'd get more mail if you wrote more letters."

"I suppose you have a point there," George said sullenly.

Christy thanked Mr. Pentland, then joined George and Creed.

"So, how are we coming here?"

Creed beamed up at her. "I think I got it whopped, Miz Christy. If'n I got me four magic rabbits and eight magic rabbits, and I put 'em all in a big ol' hat, well, then, I'll have me twelve magic rabbits."

"That's right, Creed!" Christy said.

"I'll have me a passel o' baby rabbits, too, sooner 'n you can blink an eye," Creed said. "That is, if magic rabbits are anything like the ones that live around these here parts."

Christy glanced at George. "Magic rabbits?"

"I thought it might make the problem more interesting. It's no fun adding apples or stones. But magic rabbits, now, *they're* interesting!"

"Well, I guess the important thing is that it worked," Christy said grudgingly. "Thanks, George."

"He's a fine teacher, Miz Christy," Creed said.

"Yes, I guess he is."

Christy started for her desk. For a moment, hot tears stung her eyes. She always tried to make her lessons as fun and interesting as possible, she told herself. Just because George had come up with an inventive approach didn't mean she wasn't a fine teacher.

And yet . . . once again, there it was—the green-eyed monster.

"Sis?" George was right behind her. "Everything all right?"

Christy forced a smile. "Just fine. I was thinking about . . . about monsters, actually."

"Hmm. They might work even better than the magic rabbits."

"Maybe so."

George pointed to the letter in the pocket of Christy's sweater. "I was wondering. You plan on reading that?"

"Eventually. I usually wait until evening to read my letters. I like to save them. It gives me something to look forward to."

George lunged toward Christy and grabbed the letter.

He raced around the room holding the letter high in the air, taunting her. A few of the children started to giggle.

Christy was irritated, but more than that she didn't like the serious look that filled George's eyes. She couldn't help feeling that this was not a joke.

"George," she yelled, "it's my letter!"

"Mine," he said as he bounced merrily about the room.

"George, give me the letter" she said firmly.

Reluctantly George stopped and handed her the letter.

She shrugged. "I know it sounds silly. But around here, a letter is a big event."

"I was just curious to see how Mother and Father are doing. Maybe I could read it now, but not tell you what it says—"

"No, George!" Christy cried. "It wouldn't be the same at all. Half the fun of getting a letter is opening the envelope. It's like a present. You can read it when I'm done."

George looked annoyed, but Christy didn't much care. He was already taking over her friends and her job. The least he could do was let her enjoy her precious letter.

He started to turn away, but Christy touched his arm. "Thanks," she said.

"For what?"

"For helping with Creed. Maybe you should consider going into teaching."

George gave a strange, faraway smile. "I have a pretty good feeling my future's not heading in that direction," he said darkly. And with that, he left.

❧ Seven ❧

Y ou're awfully quiet," Christy said to George.

"I'm just concentrating on not falling off the side of this mountain," he replied.

It was late afternoon, and the two of them were heading for the doctor's cabin. Christy was riding Prince, the mission's black stallion. George was on Goldie, Miss Alice's palomino.

The path to the doctor's was narrow but well-worn. By now, Christy was used to the sheer drop-offs and craggy peaks. But she was being careful to keep the pace slow, for George's sake. He'd seemed preoccupied on the trip—no doubt because of the steep trail. In any case, there was no point in rushing. It was a beautiful afternoon, a time to savor the rustle of the birch and hemlock and the musical rush of the mountain brooks.

"The children missed you this afternoon," Christy said. "Where'd you go?"

"Oh, just wandering," George said softly. "Taking in the sights. Thinking deep thoughts." He paused as Goldie stepped gingerly over a fallen log. "I hope I wasn't out of line today."

"Out of line?"

"You know. Trying to teach Creed. It's not like I knew what I was doing. You're the teacher. I'm not."

Christy glanced over her shoulder and smiled at George. "Well, I have to admit I was a little miffed. I've had such a hard time getting through to Creed, and then you step in with your magic rabbits, and *presto*— Everything's fine."

"Beginner's luck. Believe me, Sis, you're a great teacher." He sighed. "I wish there were more teachers like you at the Bristol Academy. You treat the children like real people. Not just scores on a piece of paper."

"Aren't there any teachers you like?"

"Oh, some are all right. But the headmaster, Mr. Koller . . . he's the worst."

Christy was surprised at the bitterness in her brother's voice. "What do you mean?"

George hesitated. "Oh, don't listen to me. You know I love to complain. Hey, up ahead— is that the doctor's cabin?"

"I told you I'd get you there in one piece."

"Now, if you can just get me back to the mission intact."

As they tied up the horses, Doctor MacNeill came to the door. "Welcome!" he cried, waving the spoon he held in his right hand. "You're just in time to help."

As usual, his cabin was a mess. The kitchen table was covered with a hodgepodge of medical books and glass bottles filled with drugs. The bookcase was layered with dust. Still, the cabin was a comfortable place. The air was sweet with something Christy couldn't quite identify.

"Shall I take your sweater?" the doctor asked.

"Thanks," Christy said, "it's warm in here."

"I've been cooking all day. That smell," the doctor said proudly, "is my very own rendition of rabbit stew. I got the original recipe from Granny O'Teale."

"Granny?" Christy asked doubtfully. Granny O'Teale was known for her strange mountain potions and herbs. Who knew what her recipe for rabbit stew would taste like?

"Have you ever made this before?"

The doctor grinned. "Trust me. I'm a chef at heart," the doctor assured her.

Then turning his attention to her brother, he asked, "What about you, George? Ever done any cooking?"

"I used to lick the spoon when Mother made chocolate frosting."

Doctor MacNeill passed him a wooden spoon. "Let's put your talents to the test. Go ahead and stir up that pot, would you?"

"What about me?" Christy asked.

"You can clear off the table and set it," the doctor instructed, "if you're feeling brave."

While Christy and George went to work, the doctor began making biscuits. Doctor MacNeill and Christy chatted away, but George remained distant and preoccupied— nothing like his usual buoyant self.

"So, George," the doctor said, "I think you have the makings of a fine chef."

"Today I told him he should consider a teaching career," Christy added.

"What is it you want to do for a living someday?" the doctor asked George. "Have you given it any thought?"

George shrugged. "I'd like to work for a newspaper, I think. You know—dig up stories, write on deadline. Maybe in New York, some big city like that." He looked out the window at the setting sun. "You don't even really need an education for that, I expect."

"Of course you do!" Christy exclaimed. "I'm sure they prefer to hire someone who's been to college."

"I used to know a guy named Jack O'Dell who wrote for the *New York Times*," Doctor

41

MacNeill said. "His brother and I went to medical school together. Jack started out as a paperboy for the *Times*. Hung around the place so much they let him start writing obituaries. Before you know it, he had by-lines on the front page nearly every day."

George seemed to brighten. "That's what I'm saying. I could do the same thing, if I wanted to. Start at the bottom, work myself up the ladder."

"George," Christy asked, eyeing her brother, "you're not thinking of quitting school—"

"No, no. Of course not. Can't you just see Mother's face if I did something that stupid?"

"Not to mention Father's," Christy added.

"Anyway, if all else fails and I can't be a writer, I'll always have a promising career as a magician," George joked.

"Better that than a chef," the doctor said, grabbing the spoon from George as the stew threatened to boil over.

＊＊＊

Before long, Christy and George were sitting down at the table while the doctor ladled out large portions of his stew into bowls. When he sat down, he asked George to give thanks.

"Well, what are you waiting for?" the doctor asked expectantly after the prayer. "Dig in!"

"Ladies first," George said with mock politeness then grinned at his sister.

"No, no," Christy replied. "I insist you have the honor, George. After all, you're our guest. And I'm anxious to see what you think of a real, live mountain recipe. Granny O'Teale is known for her, uh . . . original approach to dining."

The doctor scowled. He sat down and scooped up a heaping spoonful of stew from his own bowl.

"Mmm," he murmured as he swallowed down the stew. A look of pure delight crossed his face. "Ambrosia. A meal fit for a king, if I do say so myself."

George took a deep breath. He dipped his spoon timidly into the rich, strange-smelling broth. "Oh, well," he said. "What's the worst that could happen?"

"You could die a slow and agonizing death," Christy replied with a straight face. "Fortunately, there's a doctor on hand."

Together, Christy and George each took a tiny bite of stew. Their eyes met in surprise.

"It . . . it's actually good!" Christy cried.

"Wonderful," George agreed.

Doctor MacNeill leaned back in his chair, arms crossed over his chest. "Oh, ye of little faith," he chided. "And what exactly did you expect?"

Christy just smiled in reply. "Pass the salt," she said, winking at George.

"Don't worry about cleaning up, George," Doctor MacNeill said again. "I'll take care of things after you leave. Just sit out here on the porch with Christy and me. It's a beautiful night. The stars are putting on quite a show."

"Oh, I don't mind," George said as he headed back into the cabin. "It's the least I can do after such a gourmet feast."

"Was that a hint of sarcasm I heard?" the doctor inquired.

"Not a bit," George said. "I loved the stew. As a matter of fact, the rabbit I use in my magic tricks may not be long for this world!"

"George, would you mind getting my sweater?" Christy asked. "It's getting a little chilly out here."

"Not at all."

As George retrieved Christy's sweater, he pulled out the letter from their Mother that was in the pocket. Would he have time to read it? And what if Christy noticed it was missing?

What does it matter now? he silently asked himself. *Getting caught reading a letter is the least of my worries.*

He slipped the letter into his shirt pocket and returned to the porch. "Here you go."

"Thanks, George," Christy said as she put on the sweater. She smiled at the doctor. "He didn't used to be so well-behaved."

"It's just an act for the doc's benefit," George said. "Now, you two sit tight. I'll be out in a minute after I get everything cleaned up."

Back in the cabin, George made a show of clearing off the kitchen table. Out on the porch, Christy and the doctor were deep in conversation.

If he wanted to know what was in that note, now was his chance.

George placed the doctor's teakettle back on the fire. When it started to steam, he held the envelope over the hot mist, just long enough for the wax seal on the back to loosen. He slipped a knife under the seal and it opened without cracking.

Carefully, he removed the sheets inside. *My dearest Christy,* the letter began. *I'm afraid I have some terrible news.*

‽ Eight ‽

George took a deep breath. He glanced over his shoulder. Out on the porch, the doctor was whispering something in Christy's ear. He turned back to the letter and read on:

> We have just received very disturbing news from George's school. I will recount the story to you as briefly as I can, and then you will see why your father and I are worried so about your brother.
>
> It seems that recently a large sum of money was stolen from the headmaster's office. Two students saw George and his roommate, Richard, in the vicinity of the office the evening that the money disappeared. When confronted about this, George instantly confessed to stealing the money.
>
> As awful as that is, there is more.

*The next morning, George was
summoned to the headmaster's office.
But instead of appearing, he simply
vanished without a trace! His suitcase is gone, along with a few clothes
and belongings. He has not been
sighted since—and this was several
days ago.*

"George?" Christy called. "Are you ever
coming out to join us?"

"In a minute. I'm almost done in here. You
two just relax. I may be slow but I'm extremely thorough. It's been so long since I've
cleaned up, I've almost forgotten how."

"All right. But we should be getting home
before too much longer."

George turned to the next page. His
mother's careful handwriting had grown
more frantic. And some of the words were
blurred, by tears no doubt:

*In his letter, the headmaster expressed
his sorrow and anger about this inci-
dent. He had intended to expel George.
After all, in this situation, what choice
did he really have? But he did say that
although he had often found your
brother to be "a tad exuberant," he
would be sorely missed. He seemed
genuinely shocked at this turn of*

*events—no more so, of course, than are
your father and I.*

*Dear, have you had any word at
all from your brother? I know how
much he looks up to you. Perhaps
he's contacted you by now.*

*I've tried to call you at the mission,
but the operator tells me the new
phone line is down for repairs. So I
am sending this letter off in the hopes
that you will write or call with news.*

*As you can imagine, we are beside
ourselves with worry. We've even tried
contacting your Aunt Lucy and
Grandmother and Grandfather
Huddleston. We didn't want to
worry them, so we tried to give them
as few details as possible.*

*I lie awake nights wondering how
this could possibly have happened,
Christy. George is such a good boy.
What would possess him to steal
money? Could it have been a dare, or
some kind of pressure from the other
boys? Could he need money and have
been afraid to ask us?*

*Somehow, I think not. I know
George has been accused of theft,
but somehow I can't believe he is
actually guilty. I know my son. He
may have high spirits, but he is*

honest.And if he didn't take the money, he couldn't have had much spending money. How far could he have gotten? And what if he's distraught?

Your father is deeply worried, but as I do, he also believes in George.

I must end this now, as the postman will be coming soon. As soon as you receive this, please call or write us without delay.

> Love,
> Mother

George wiped away a tear. Carefully, he refolded the letter and placed it in its envelope.

Again he held the wax seal over the doctor's teakettle. It softened enough for him to reseal the envelope, although the "H" imprint his mother had made with her wax stamp was gone. Hopefully, Christy wouldn't notice. And if she did, what would it really matter?

As George finished cleaning up, he cemented his plans. He would leave early in the morning before anyone else was up. He had enough money for a one-way ticket to New York City. Of course, when he arrived, he'd be flat broke.

But he was a quick thinker. He'd get a job selling papers, like that friend of the doctor's. Or he'd perform magic tricks on the street for spare change. He'd find a way to get by. He'd have to.

Now his main concern was how to sneak the letter back into Christy's pocket. He feared she would miss it soon. He considered a dozen different options before finally deciding the simplest solution could be the best.

George returned to the porch. "Hey, Sis," he said, "I found this on the floor. Must've dropped out when I got your sweater."

"Mother's letter! I completely forgot about it. I'm glad you found it. I'd have had to ride all the way back here to retrieve it."

"I would have brought it to you," the doctor said. "It would have provided an excellent excuse to see you."

"Neil, you know you don't need an excuse to visit."

"I'm happy to report that I've also finished cleaning up," George interrupted. "At least, as clean as I'm capable of making it, which is probably not saying much. Thanks, Doc, for a great meal." He made a show of yawning.

"We really should be going." Christy stood. "It's a long way back, and it's slow going if we wait till it gets dark."

The doctor shook George's hand. "I'll be passing by the mission in a couple of days, George. You'll still be around, won't you?"

"I . . . yes, I suppose so."

"Well, I'll see you then."

"If I don't see you for some reason," George said, "I just want to say . . . well, I just want to say I think you and Christy make a great pair."

"As it happens, so do I," said the doctor. He gave Christy a gentle kiss on her forehead. "And thanks for the vote of confidence. But I'm sure I'll see you. Maybe you can even teach me one of those magic tricks of yours."

"Maybe so," George said softly. *But don't count on it*, he added silently in his thoughts.

◄ Nine ◄

I'm heading straight to bed," Christy said as she and George entered the mission house.

"Me, too. It's been a long day."

At the top of the stairs, George paused. "I just want you to know . . . well, I just want you to know that it's been great seeing you, Sis. I'm really proud of what you're doing here."

"That means a lot to me. I'm proud of you, too."

George scowled. "What have I ever done? Pulled a rabbit out of a hat? Told a few old jokes? You're doing important work here. You were wrong when you said I had the makings of a teacher today."

"But you do." Christy hesitated. "The truth is, I think the children would prefer you to me, given the choice. I have to admit, I've been a little jealous."

"Jealous? Of me?" George scoffed. "That's a laugh. Besides, teaching isn't about being entertaining for an afternoon. It's about having patience, day after day after day. And it's about trusting your students . . ." George's voice seemed to catch, "about having faith in them. That's what you do that's so important."

"Thanks, George." Christy gave her brother a long hug. "But this doesn't mean you're getting out of helping with the children's arithmetic class tomorrow."

"'Night, Sis."

"Goodnight."

Christy closed her bedroom door. She felt better, having admitted her feelings to George. And he'd said just the right things to help.

He really was getting more mature, she reflected. He was turning into quite a wonderful young man.

She took off her sweater and noticed the letter from her mother. She was so tired. Maybe she should save the letter for tomorrow, when she could enjoy it. Perhaps she'd read it out loud to George at breakfast.

In the meantime, her bed was looking extremely inviting.

It only took a few minutes for George to pack his bag—after all, there wasn't much to pack. He was relieved when he found some paper and a pencil in the top drawer of his dresser. But when he started to write a note to Christy, he realized he had absolutely no idea what to say.

What could he possibly write? That he was sorry? That he hoped Christy would understand he was really a good person, despite everything? That he hoped she and his parents would someday find it in their hearts to forgive him?

It all sounded so lame when he considered the torment of his mother's letter—the tears, the heartbreak. Were there any words in the English language to make pain like that go away?

George chewed on the end of the pencil. He could almost hear his English teacher, Mr. Drake, chiding him for the hundredth time, "Pencils are for writing one's most profound thoughts, Master Huddleston. They are not food for human consumption."

Old Mr. Drake. George would never see him again.

Now that he was leaving school behind for good, George had begun to realize just how much he'd enjoyed it. He might not have been the best student, but he liked learning. He liked his friends. In his own way, he even liked old Mr. Drake.

The blank page stared up at him. What could he write?

Well, at least he could try to write the truth:

Dear Christy:
All I can say is that I love you.
And that I'm sorry.

George

It wasn't the best letter in the world. But it was the best he could do.

———

He tried to sleep, but of course, he couldn't. He was dressed and ready to leave by the time the first pale pink tendrils of dawn made their appearance.

Carrying his suitcase, George slipped into the hallway and tiptoed down the stairs. Halfway down, he thought he heard someone in the hallway.

He paused, holding his breath. Nothing.

George ran the rest of the way down the stairs. He'd just grabbed the front door handle when he heard a voice.

"George? Where are you a-runnin' off to?"

George spun around. There stood Ruby Mae in the pale light. She was wearing a threadbare robe and an exasperated expression on her face.

"Ruby Mae! What on earth are you doing up at this hour?"

"I heard you a-sneakin' around." She crossed her arms over her chest. "So, where are you goin'?"

"Me? I'm not going anywhere."

"You're not goin' anywhere with your suitcase? Looks mighty strange to me."

"This? Oh, this just . . . uh, this has my magic tricks in it. Christy asked me if I'd do a little demonstration at school today. I was just taking my things over to get it all set up."

"You're a-goin' to do more magic for us?"

"Yep," George replied. Seeing Ruby Mae's thrilled expression, he couldn't help but feel guilty. But he was in this deep. And he had to escape without her waking Christy.

"I'll come with you," Ruby Mae said.

"Oh, no. You can't do that."

"But why? I could be your . . . what's that word? Your assister?"

"Assistant. That would be great. But I can't have anyone actually see how I set up my tricks. Then it wouldn't be magic anymore, don't you see?"

"You showed Creed how to make paper flowers. And you done showed everyone how to pull things outa ears."

"But a magician can't give away all his tricks. What fun would that be?"

Ruby Mae grimaced. "Can I at least be your assistant today at school?"

"I'd be delighted," George said. "Now, you go back to sleep. I'll see you soon."

He watched as Ruby Mae, grinning happily at her new assistant assignment, rushed back up the stairs. Quietly, George closed the front door behind him.

He hated lying like this. He hated leaving like this.

He'd thought he couldn't feel any worse about himself. But he was wrong.

❧ Ten ❦

I get to be George's assistant today," Ruby Mae announced when Christy came downstairs that morning.

Christy joined Ruby Mae, Miss Ida, and Miss Alice at the dining room table. "His assistant?" she repeated as she ladled oatmeal into a bowl.

"For when he does the magic tricks."

Christy frowned. "I'm afraid I don't know what you're talking about, Ruby Mae. Where is George, anyway? Is he up yet?"

"He was up at the crack o' dawn," Ruby Mae said. "I guess he had a lot of gettin' ready to do for the magic show."

"You saw him this morning?"

"He was just headin' out the door with his suitcase. That's when he told me I could be his assistant. I hope I get to wear a costume."

Christy glanced at Miss Alice. "Did you say *suitcase?*"

"He puts all his tricks in there. He was takin' 'em over to the school."

"I think I'd better check on this." Christy pushed back her chair. She had an icy lump in the pit of her stomach. George had been so quiet yesterday evening. And now, here was this story about him sneaking out the door at dawn, carrying a suitcase. She had a bad feeling.

With Ruby Mae at her heels, Christy ran across the dewy yard to the schoolhouse. Nervously, she pushed open the door.

"B—but there ain't nobody here!" Ruby Mae cried.

Ruby Mae ran to the front of the room, checking everywhere for a sign of George or his magic tricks. But after a few minutes, she turned to Christy, defeated.

"I don't understand," she said.

"I'm afraid I don't, either, Ruby Mae," Christy said.

Back at the mission house, Christy and Ruby Mae hurriedly headed straight upstairs to George's room.

Christy knocked softly on his door. No answer. Slowly she opened it. His bed was neatly made. His dresser was empty.

"He left a note!" Ruby Mae exclaimed.

Christy read the simple letter. "What does

it mean?" she wondered aloud. "What is he sorry about?"

Ruby Mae scowled. "For runnin' off without even sayin' his goodbyes proper-like, I reckon. And to think I was hopin' to marry him someday! Your brother ain't the least bit reliable, Miz Christy. If'n you don't mind my sayin' so."

"George is a little unpredictable sometimes," Christy admitted, "but he's never done anything like this before."

They returned to the dining room. "So?" Miss Alice asked. "What's the verdict?"

"I don't know what a verdict is," Ruby Mae snapped, "but I'll tell you this much—there ain't goin' to be no magic show today. Not unless you count George disappearin'."

"He's gone," Miss Ida cried, "without saying goodbye?"

"It looks that way," Christy said. "He left me a note, but I don't really understand what it means," Christy passed the letter to Miss Alice.

"But George is such a polite boy—so charming." Miss Ida clucked her tongue. "This just doesn't seem like him."

"It isn't," Christy agreed. "That's why I'm worried."

Miss Alice stared at the note. "Was anything bothering George?" she asked. "Perhaps a problem at school? A girlfriend?"

"Girlfriend!" Ruby Mae cried. "George was sweet on somebody?"

"Not that I know of, Ruby Mae," Christy said.

Miss Alice patted Christy's arm. "I'm sure there's a logical explanation, dear. He's probably heading back to the station at El Pano. Why don't you take Prince and go look for him?"

"But what about school?"

"David and I will take care of teaching today. You'll do everyone a lot more good by getting to the bottom of this mystery."

Christy gave her a hug. "Thank you, Miss Alice. I'm just going to run upstairs and get my sweater, and I'll be on my way."

"I'll fix you up a sandwich for the road," Miss Ida volunteered.

"Thanks, Miss Ida. That would be great." Christy hesitated. "Would you mind making two? Just in case I can talk George into coming back?"

"Of course. You just tell that boy we expect him at dinner this evening, promptly at six."

"And tell him his assistant is mad as a wildcat that he up and left without doin' a magic show," Ruby Mae added.

Christy managed a smile. "I will, Ruby Mae."

She ran upstairs, two steps at a time. There

had to be a logical explanation. There just *had* to be.

Christy donned her sweater. She was starting down the stairs when she felt the envelope from her mother in her pocket. She pulled out the letter and returned it to her dresser. She didn't want to risk losing it on her ride.

As she set it down, she noticed something strange about the wax seal on the back. Her mother's usual initial imprint was gone, as if it had melted. And the wax was barely sticking to the envelope.

Suddenly, she pictured George, bringing her the letter at the doctor's cabin last night.

Something was very wrong here.

Christy slipped her finger under the seal and pulled out her mother's letter.

My dearest Christy, she read. *I'm afraid I have some terrible news.*

Her heart in her throat, Christy read on. When she was done, she wiped away a tear.

Now at least, George's recent actions made more sense to her. He had come to Cutter Gap to hide from their parents and the school's headmaster.

Christy began to examine her beliefs about her brother. *It isn't like George to steal, but it also isn't like him to read other people's mail*, she thought.

Christy wasn't sure whether to be angry at George or to be compassionate about his situation. Either way, she knew only part of the reason for George's sudden disappearance, and she knew she was going to find him to hear his side of the story. *George may not know it,* she thought, *but he needs his big sister right now.*

✑ Eleven ✑

Well, I have to admit it doesn't look good," David said as he helped Christy saddle up Prince.

She'd shown David her mother's letter. He'd read it twice before reacting.

"I keep thinking there must be more to the story," Christy said, but she could hear the desperation in her own voice. "Hoping, anyway."

David spread a blanket over Prince's broad back. "The thing is, he ran away, Christy. If he didn't take the money, why would George have run?"

"I've asked myself that, too. And I don't have an answer." Christy rubbed her eyes. She was already tired, and the day had just begun. "But why would George steal money, David? Father sends him an allowance. George has always had everything he needed."

David shrugged. "Who knows? Maybe he had a girlfriend he wanted to impress. Maybe he owed someone money and couldn't pay it all back. There could be a hundred reasons. In the end, it doesn't really matter what his reason was. What matters is that he did something wrong, and now he has to face up to the consequences like a man."

"He's a good person, David. A little impetuous, to be sure. But I know he has a good heart."

David positioned Prince's saddle. "Why don't I ride with you, Christy? You're in no mood to be alone right now. And Miss Alice can handle school today."

"No. You have plenty of other work to do."

"You don't even know what direction he headed."

"It's a pretty safe guess he's going back toward El Pano. At least, that's as good a place to start as any. And in any case, George is my brother. This is my problem."

David patted her shoulder. "The truth is, it's George's problem, Christy. He's the one who made the mistake. And only he can correct it."

"First of all, I believe in my brother. He would not steal. And think how alone he must feel right now. He's afraid to go home. He's afraid to go back to school. And he's afraid to come back here." Tears burned her eyes. "I know things don't look good for George right now. That's why he *needs* a friend more than ever. He needs me."

———

How could the morning be so beautiful, Christy wondered, when she felt so gloomy?

The trail to El Pano snaked through the mountains past rocky chasms and sheer cliffs. Swift-moving streams followed much of the route. The thin path was covered with a thick canopy of trees. Patches of sunlight dappled the forest floor.

Christy tried to occupy herself with other thoughts. For a while, she identified wildflowers that her friend, Fairlight Spencer, had shown her.

But always her thoughts strayed back to George. And always the questions remained. Why had he done such a thing? And why had he run away—from school, and then from her?

Minutes passed, slowly turning into hours. The sun was high in the sky now. After a while, Christy found a shady spot by a pair of birch trees. She stopped there and decided to eat the sandwich Miss Ida had prepared. But as soon as she unwrapped the sandwich, she realized she wasn't the least bit hungry.

Something was wrong. She should have

passed George by now. Even giving him a good head start, she had the advantage of a swift horse. For someone walking with a suitcase, this would be a tedious and tiring route.

Perhaps she'd been wrong to think George would come this way. How did she know what he was thinking? After all, she would never have dreamed he would get himself into this kind of trouble. Who knew where he was heading next?

With a sigh, Christy wrapped up her uneaten sandwich after giving the vegetables to Prince. She wondered how much farther she should travel. If she went all the way to El Pano, she'd never get back to the mission today.

Another hour, she promised herself. Another hour, and then she would give up.

"Christy."

The voice came from behind her on the path. For a moment, Christy froze. She thought it sounded like him, but sound in these woods could be distorted. And there were plenty of unsavory types lurking in the forest.

Slowly, she turned her head.

As if by magic, George stepped out of the woods.

"Hey, Sis," he said softly.

"But . . . how could I have missed you? Did I ride right past you?"

George gave a sheepish grin. "I heard you

coming and I hid in some bushes. Then I started having second thoughts."

Christy stared at her brother. He was in the middle of the path, his suitcase tightly clutched in his right hand. Standing here in the middle of this vast forest, he looked surprisingly small, like a little boy. His hair was mussed. He had a scratch on one cheek. His clothes were wrinkled.

He looked so vulnerable—not at all like the cocky, self-confident George of a few days ago. He looked lost.

He looked like someone who needed a big sister.

Christy walked to his side. She put her arms around his shoulders and pulled him close. He stiffened, then relented. With a sigh, he rested his head on her shoulder.

"Oh, Sis," he whispered, "I've really made a mess of things, haven't I?"

"Maybe I can help," Christy whispered, "if you let me."

"Nobody can help. It's too late."

"It's never too late. Not if you pray for God to guide you through this."

George looked at her pleadingly. The desperation in his eyes was almost more than she could bear.

"George," Christy said sternly, "It's time for the lying to stop. Why are you *really* here in Cutter Gap?"

❧ Twelve ❧

George stared at his sister, searching his heart for the right answer. At last he said softly, "Didn't you read Mother's letter?"

"Yes. But it just made me think of a hundred questions to ask, George. It didn't give me any answers. Only you can do that."

And I'm not going to, George thought. *Not ever. I'm a man of my word, and my lips are sealed.*

"Let's start at the beginning," Christy said, using the same tone of voice she reserved for her most difficult students. "The money. Did you take the money, George?"

George kicked at a loose stone in the path. "Mother and Father seem to think I did. Don't you?"

"I don't know what to think. But I do know that you're a decent, honorable person."

"Well, even decent, honorable people make mistakes."

"But why?" Christy's blue eyes were clouded with confusion. "Why would you take money from the headmaster's office and risk everything? It just doesn't make any sense."

"Why does it matter now, Sis? What's done is done. I'm out of the academy. I can't go home."

"You can always go home, George. Mother and Father will always stand by you. And so will I."

"I don't need anyone. I'm going to New York City to become a writer."

George almost laughed at how ridiculous he sounded. He was surprised and touched when Christy didn't even smile.

"You'll make a wonderful writer someday, George. Or artist. Or—" Christy smiled, "magician. I think you can do anything you set your mind to. But you need to finish your education first."

"Well, I don't think the Bristol Academy will be welcoming me back with open arms. But sure, I'll try to go back to school someday." George threw back his shoulders and did his best to project a confident smile. "Well, I'd better be on my way. It's a long walk to El Pano."

Christy grabbed his arm. "George, whatever happened back at school, you have to face it. You can't run from your problems. They have a way of following you."

"Like my big sister?" George tried to joke.

"I can help you. I know I can, if you'll just let me."

George shook off her hand. "Christy, I'm a big boy. I can handle my own problems."

"At least let me give you a ride to El Pano. It's a long trip on foot."

"No."

Christy's face froze into a grimace of frustration. "You can be so pig-headed and stubborn and unreasonable!" she cried. "Sometimes I feel just like I did when you were a little boy. Mother would ask me to call you in for dinner, but you'd be busy playing and you'd ignore me, no matter how I pleaded."

"What can I say?" George forced a grin. "I'm your little brother. It's my job to torment you."

Just then, George heard the sound of voices, coming from beyond the next ridge. A moment later, a tall, gaunt man George recognized as Mr. Pentland appeared, carrying a small mail bag.

But it was the person walking beside him who made George's heart do a somersault.

Richard!

What was his roommate doing here? Now?

Frantically, George's eyes darted about. His

first reaction was to dive for cover, but of course, that was ridiculous.

He was trapped.

"Well, well, who do we have here?" Mr. Pentland called. "Miz Christy, I declare. Ain't often I meet up with company on this here route. And George, too!" Mr. Pentland elbowed Richard. "Seems you found him sooner 'n you figgered."

Richard and George locked eyes. Richard was a small, slight boy, with curly blond hair and wide, hopeful eyes. He was dressed in his worn brown jacket and a too-large pair of pants that had once belonged to George. Richard's family didn't have much money, and George often lent him clothes.

"Richard," George said darkly, "I should never have told you I was coming here. Why are you here? There's no point." He paused, making his next words emphatic. "*Everything is decided.*"

Richard ignored George. He approached Christy and shook her hand. "You must be George's sister. I've heard so much about you, Miss Huddleston. I'm Richard Benton, George's roommate from the Bristol Academy."

"Richard!" Christy exclaimed. "Yes, George has spoken of you. But how . . . why are you here?"

"Good question," George muttered.

"Well, that's a long story." Richard paused. "How much does she know, George?"

"She knows all she needs to know," George said. "If you have something to talk about, Richard, let's do it privately."

"Didn't you get my letter?" Richard asked.

"Yes, I got it."

"Well, then—"

"I didn't read it, Richard. I threw it in a pond without even opening it."

Richard took a step closer to George. He had a fierceness in his eyes that George had never seen before. "Look, we can talk now, in front of Christy and Mr. Pentland, or we can talk later. But we're *going* to talk, George Huddleston."

George gazed up the path, then back. All he wanted to do was run. But he was trapped. He *had* to deal with Richard. And he didn't want Christy to get caught up in the middle of everything.

"Whatever it is you two have to discuss, why don't you do it back at the mission?" Christy interjected.

George sighed deeply. "All right. One more night, and then Richard and I leave in the morning. But there's one condition."

"What's that?" his sister asked.

"No questions. All right?"

"No conditions, George," Christy replied. "You're my brother and I love you. I want to

73

help you. And if that means I have to ask some hard questions, so be it."

"All right, then." George gave her a stiff smile. "You can ask all the questions you want. But I'm not guaranteeing I'll answer any of them."

✺ Thirteen ✺

He's back!" Ruby Mae cried. "George is back!"

As Christy, George, Richard, and Mr. Pentland approached the mission house, they were met with a flurry of activity. Ruby Mae ran to greet them, and Miss Ida, Miss Alice, David, and the doctor appeared on the porch.

"Neil!" Christy exclaimed. "What are you doing here?"

"Just stopped by to check on the reviews of my dinner," the doctor said, glancing over at George. "Actually, I was running low on some medical supplies, and thought I'd see if Miss Alice had any she could spare." He paused. "It seems you found your brother."

Everyone fell silent. All eyes were on George.

He stopped in his tracks at the foot of the porch steps. "Look, I know you all are wondering what's going on," he said softly, a pained expression on his face. "I . . . all I can say is that I'm sorry I left so abruptly, especially after all your wonderful hospitality. But I don't want to talk about this. It's private." He glanced sharply at Richard. "This is Richard, my roommate from school. He and I will be leaving in the morning. Come on, Richard."

The two boys headed into the house. Ruby Mae tugged on Christy's sleeve. "What's a-goin' on, Miz Christy? Nothin' George said makes a lick o' sense. What happened?"

"I don't know, Ruby Mae," Christy said in a determined voice. "But I'm about to find out right now."

"Go away."

Christy knocked on George's door again. "We need to talk, George. I still have some questions."

"And I didn't promise you any answers."

This time, Christy pounded on George's door. He wanted to be stubborn? Well, she could be just as stubborn . . . and then some!

"I'm not leaving this hallway, George."

A moment later, George's door opened a crack. "Christy, Father always said you were the most pig-headed girl he'd ever had the privilege of knowing."

76

"Well, Mother always said you're so stubborn you could be part mule!"

George stared at his sister through the crack. Christy could see the start of a smile on his face. "You're really not going to leave me alone, are you?"

"No, I'm not."

The door swung open. Richard was staring out the window. He nodded at Christy, then returned his gaze to the beautiful mountain vistas.

Christy sat down on George's bed. "All right. I'm listening."

"Just then, you sounded exactly like Father," George said quietly. "You're not my parent, you know."

"I'm your sister, George. I love you. I'll stand by you, if you will just help me understand what's going on."

George stared at his reflection in the small mirror mounted over his dresser. "I'm a man now, Christy. I have to take responsibility for my actions."

For the first time, Richard spoke up. "I believe I'm the one who's supposed to say that line."

"What do you mean, Richard?" Christy asked, surprised.

Richard turned to face Christy. He bit on his lower lip to keep from crying. "I'm the one who's not taking responsibility for his actions."

"Richard . . ." George said in a low, warning voice.

"I have to tell her, George. I have to clear my conscience."

"Don't be a fool! The damage is already done—"

"Miss Huddleston," Richard said in a choked voice, "George didn't take that money from the headmaster's office. I did."

❧ Fourteen ❧

Y ou?" Christy exclaimed.

"Don't listen to him, Christy," George began, but Richard waved him aside.

"I'm ashamed to admit it, but yes, I'm the one," Richard said then lowered his head in shame. "I sneaked into the headmaster's office by picking the lock on his door." He shrugged. "It wasn't so hard, really."

"But I don't understand." Christy frowned. "Why did George say he took the money?"

"Because he was trying to be a good friend," Richard said. "He was wrong to cover for me that way, but he meant well." Richard slumped onto the bed next to Christy. "You see, George knew how short my family is for cash. I'm on a full scholarship at the academy." He smiled crookedly. "Even my clothes are hand-me-downs. George gave me this jacket and these pants."

"Richard," George said, his voice softened, "you don't have to tell my sister all this."

"But I *want* to, George, don't you understand? There's nothing worse than carrying around a terrible secret like this."

Christy touched Richard's shoulder. She was surprised that he was trembling. "Go on, Richard."

"Well, George figured if I were expelled for taking the money, I wouldn't ever be able to get into another school. Who's going to give a scholarship to someone who's been expelled for stealing?"

Christy looked at her brother sharply. "But doesn't the same logic apply to you?"

"Maybe." George gave one of his I-can-handle-anything smiles. "But I have a way of landing on my feet, Sis. And Richard—well, he's got a lot to deal with right now. His father worked for the railroads, but he hurt his back last year. Richard has three younger sisters, and the family's pretty hard-up for money."

Richard shook his head. "I should have quit school and gotten a job to help my family a long time ago. But my parents insisted that I finish school. They said that way I could get a good job later on, a real one." He paused, looking a little embarrassed. "I always thought I might become a doctor. You know—to help people like my father."

"I know how hard it must be for you and

your family, Richard," Christy said gently. "I've seen poverty here in Cutter Gap that I never even imagined could exist. But I'm sure you realize it doesn't justify taking money that doesn't belong to you."

Richard started to speak, but George stepped in. "Christy, Richard's little sister broke her leg a few months ago. They didn't have the money to have it set properly, and the leg didn't heal correctly. Now she's in constant pain, and the only thing that can help her is surgery."

"Surgery," Richard added, "that my father simply can't afford."

"Oh," Christy said. "I see."

"The doctors said if they had enough money for a first payment, they'd go ahead with the surgery." Richard wiped away a tear. "I thought . . . well, I know I was wrong, but I thought if I could help Abigail, it'd be worth any cost. I guess I didn't really think things through."

"I told you not to worry," George said brightly. "I've got everything under control."

"No, you don't, George. I should have listened to you that night," Richard said. He turned to Christy. "After I told George what I'd done, he tried to talk me into turning myself in. He said the headmaster would understand, and that I wouldn't be able to live with myself if I kept the money. But then the headmaster's assistant came to our dormitory door . . ."

"What did he say, Richard?"

"He said that somebody had seen George and me in the area that night. That's true, Miss Huddleston. I told him I wanted to take a walk, and he headed back to our room. But George didn't have any idea what I was planning. George is completely innocent. You have to believe me."

Christy glanced at her brother. "I do."

"And when George spoke up and said *he'd* taken the money, I just went numb," Richard continued. "After he left, I wrote him here, since he'd told me this was where he was heading first. I told him how badly I felt about everything."

"But what's done is done, Richard," George said. "I'm going off to New York City to seek my fame and fortune, and you, my friend, are going to go straight back to school. Someday, I'll be a famous writer and you'll be a famous doctor, and we'll get together over dinner and laugh about all this."

George's words hung in the air. Richard slowly shook his head. "No, George. That's not what's going to happen. What is going to happen is that I'm going to go back to school—with you—to tell everyone the truth."

"And what about Abigail?" George quickly shot back.

Richard didn't have an answer, but Christy did.

"If Abigail loves her brother as much as I love mine," she said, "then I don't think she'd want him to make this kind of sacrifice for her."

"There's no point in going back," George argued. "The headmaster won't let me off. He'll say that since I knew about Richard's crime, I should have turned him in right then and there instead of covering for him."

"But you tried to talk me into turning myself in!" Richard cried.

"It doesn't matter." George shook his head. "What point is there in both of us getting expelled? This way, at least you'll have a chance to finish school."

"I can't let you do that," Richard replied. "Besides the truth will come out anyway when I return the money."

"You have to tell the truth and clear the air, George," Christy said. "It's the only way. I'll go with you, if you like."

George hung his head. "This is all such a mess. I just wanted to help. . . ."

"Things might just work out better than you've imagined," Christy said. "You never know. I've seen some real miracles since moving here to Cutter Gap."

"I don't know, Sis. I think it's too late. I don't think I can go back there now. I couldn't face everyone after all the lies I told. Especially Mother and Father."

"Trust me, George. I'll help you get through this." She squeezed his hand. "Remember that leap into the water I took, back when we were children? Well, it's time for *your* leap of faith."

❧ Fifteen ❧

Personally, Christy," said Miss Ida, "I don't see why you're going to the academy with your brother. After what he did, perhaps he should face the music himself."

Dinner was over, and Richard and George were upstairs. By now, everyone knew the whole story, which Christy had explained. All through dinner, Richard and George had sat quietly, avoiding all eyes. The conversation had been polite, except for a few intrusive questions from Ruby Mae. Still, both boys had barely touched their food.

But now that Richard and George were safely out of earshot, everyone seemed to have an opinion to share with Christy.

"Seems to me when a young man lies to his own flesh and blood, the last thing he deserves is a second chance," Miss Ida said as she cleared the dining room table.

"But George meant well, Miss Ida," Christy argued. "I'm not defending the fact that he wasn't honest with us, but he did mean well."

Miss Ida clucked her tongue. "That boy deserves to be punished, if you ask me."

Christy went out onto the porch, where David, the doctor, and Miss Alice were sitting. "Miss Ida thinks I'm being too gentle with George," she told them. "How about the rest of you?"

"Well, as it happens, we were just discussing that very matter," said the doctor.

Christy leaned against the porch railing. The wind was gentle on her face, and sweet with pine. "And what was your conclusion?"

"In the end, the only thing that matters is *your* conclusion, Christy," said Miss Alice.

"I just keep thinking of Luke 6:31," Christy said softly. "'As ye would that men should do to you, do ye also to them likewise.' If I were in George's shoes, I would want him to stand by me at a time like this. After all, I'm his sister. I love him." She looked at Miss Alice. "Isn't that what it all comes down to?"

Miss Alice smiled her lovely, luminous smile. "I think you've already answered your own question."

━ ◆ ━ ◆ ━

The next day they reached El Pano after a long, tiring walk. After spending the night at a boarding house, Christy insisted that they stop at the general store first thing the next morning.

"Shouldn't we be going straight to the train station?" George asked, consulting his pocket watch.

"We have plenty of time," Christy said. "Not much money, but plenty of time."

"I promise I'm going to pay you and George back every cent you're lending me," Richard vowed.

"Don't you worry about it," Christy replied. "We're glad to help."

Richard wrung his hands together. "I already owe you and George so much. And Doctor MacNeill, too. Did I tell you he said he was going to make some inquiries about my sister's surgery? He said he had some doctor friends who might be able to help."

"He also said not to get your hopes up," George reminded him gently.

"Still, for him to even try . . . well, it's awfully nice of him."

"So," George said to Christy, "did you want to buy something here at the store?"

Christy pointed to the telephone in the corner of the cramped store.

"Not buy. Call. Miss Alice told me that the owner will let us use their telephone, since the one at the mission isn't working."

"A call?"

"To Mother and Father."

George took a step backward. "I can't do that, Christy."

"You have to. Mother and Father are worried sick about you."

"They're more angry than worried." George looked past her. "I . . . I'm not like you, Christy. You're the one they're always proud of. The one they can count on. Me, I'm just the family clown."

Christy couldn't help smiling. "You know what's ironic, George? That's just the reason I've always been so jealous of you—because everybody always likes you."

"I don't suppose you'd be interested in trading personalities?" George asked.

"Call Mother and Father, George. Richard and I will wait right here."

George took a deep breath. "You're not going to let me get out of this, are you?"

"No."

"What if I say the wrong thing?"

"You won't. Just tell them the truth, and the rest will fall into place."

George walked stiffly over to the phone. After speaking with the operator for a moment, he paused. He glanced over at Christy and sent her a forced, tense smile.

A moment later, Christy heard him say just the right thing:

"Hello, Mother? It's me, George. I . . . I'm sorry I made you worry. And I love you."

❧ Sixteen ❧

It's so beautiful," Christy whispered, thinking of the more modest Flora College, in Red Springs, North Carolina, where she'd gotten her training to be a teacher.

George smiled wryly at his sister. "That's because you're on the outside, looking in. When you're sitting in a classroom, agonizing over one of Mr. Burns's Latin exams, it doesn't seem quite so charming."

They were standing outside the tall bronze gate at the entrance to the Bristol Academy. The school itself was a huge white mansion surrounded by manicured grounds. Four separate dormitory buildings flanked it on either side.

"How do we get inside?" Christy asked.

"The guard will let us in," Richard replied. "At least, I *think* he will. Could be George and I are considered criminals by now."

"I still say we should have made an appointment," George argued. It was a lame attempt to stall, but he figured it was worth a try.

"I'm sure the headmaster will be anxious to hear what you have to say," Christy said.

George gazed up at the imposing main building. "I don't know, Sis. I have a bad feeling about this."

"What did Mother and Father tell you to do when you spoke to them?" Christy asked.

"Well, mostly Mother just cried," George said, still stinging at the memory. "And Father didn't have much to say. You know how he is—he just said he was confident I'd do the right thing. But I'm just not sure this *is* the right thing. If we keep our mouths shut, at least we can be sure that Richard will stay in school. This way, I'm afraid we'll both get expelled, and what good will that do?"

Richard held up the small fabric satchel he was carrying. "You're forgetting one thing— the money I stole. One way or another, George, I'm giving it back."

"You could just leave it by the headmaster's door in the middle of the night," George suggested. "No one would ever know how it got there."

"George," Christy said firmly, hands on her hips, "you're stalling."

"That's right. I am." George grinned

sheepishly. "And I was very much hoping you wouldn't notice."

"I'm sure this is the right thing to do," Christy said. "But in the end, it must be your decision."

George looked from his sister to Richard and back again. "Well, I can see I'm outnumbered." He turned to Richard. "Come on, pal. Let's get this over with, before I lose my nerve."

———

"Well, well, well. This is a surprise."

Even sitting behind his desk, Mr. Koller was an imposing man. Beefy and balding, he had a thick mustache and a deep baritone voice that seemed to shake the walls.

His office, too, was intimidating. Three walls were lined to the ceiling with leather-bound books, and Mr. Koller's mahogany desk seemed as large as a new Ford automobile. The family photograph on his desk was the only sign of a gentler man.

George had only been here once before, when he'd enrolled at the academy. His parents had been with him then. Their proud faces were etched in his memory.

It burned to think of the pain he'd heard in their voices today—the hurt and betrayal. How could he have let them down so badly? He'd meant well, of course. But it was frightening to think that you could try to do the right thing, and still end up in such an awful mess.

"And to what do I owe the honor of this visit?" Mr. Koller inquired, arms crossed over his chest.

"I . . . we . . . well, George and I have something to say," Richard began in a thin, halting voice.

"I'm all ears."

Richard and George exchanged looks. Richard was trembling. His face was ashen.

"Might this have something to do with the mystery of the vanishing money?" Mr. Koller leaned forward, elbows on his desk. He fixed his stare on George. "And the mystery of Master Huddleston's sudden and inexplicable disappearance shortly thereafter?"

"Yes," George said. "It's about the money. You see, there's been . . . well, a bit of a misunderstanding about all that."

"A misunderstanding. Is that what it's called now? You break in to my office, steal from this academy, and then call it a misunderstanding?" Mr. Koller bellowed.

George swallowed hard as Mr. Koller stared sternly at the two of them. "My word . . . What's next? What are—"

"I took it!" Richard blurted, placing the sack of money on the headmaster's desk. "I took it! George didn't. If you're going to expel anybody, it ought to be me!"

The words came out in a terrible rush. When Richard was done, he almost looked relieved.

"It's a little more complicated than that," George began, but Mr. Koller interrupted.

"Yes, it always is," he said sarcastically. He pursed his lips, gazing at Richard skeptically, as if he didn't quite believe he was capable of the crime. "And how exactly did you get into my office, if you don't mind my asking? Just so I can prevent any further incursions."

"I picked the lock," Richard admitted. "I used a piece of wire. Took a while, but I got it eventually."

"Yes, indeed, you did."

Mr. Koller leaned back in his chair, regarding each boy thoughtfully. It was impossible to tell what he was thinking. A slight smile seemed to lurk behind that mustache, but it could just as easily have been a sneer. Still, he didn't seem all *that* angry. No books had been thrown, no threats had been made. Perhaps he was going to go lightly on the boys, chalk it up to a silly prank and nothing more.

"The thing is," George spoke up, "Richard had a very good reason for taking the money, Mr. Koller. You see—"

"A good reason?" Mr. Koller repeated in a stern voice. "Are you suggesting there is ever a good reason for thievery? Do the words

'Thou shalt not steal' ring a bell for you, Master Huddleston?"

"I . . . well, of course they do. I know it's wrong to steal. And so does Richard. But sometimes there are circumstances—"

"There are *no* circumstances that justify stealing!" Mr. Koller bellowed. "And while we're on the subject, there are no circumstances that justify lying, either. Am I safe in assuming that you had knowledge of Mr. Benton's actions?"

"Yes, I did."

"But only after I'd confessed to George about what I'd done," Richard clarified. "He had nothing to do with this, Mr. Koller. You have to believe me!"

"You're asking me to believe a young man who broke into my office and stole money belonging to the academy?"

"George was only trying to protect me," Richard said weakly. "He was just trying to be a good friend."

"A good friend would have promptly turned you in to the authorities."

"George *did* try to talk me into returning the money. He did. But I was so sure I was right. . . ."

For a long time, Mr. Koller said nothing. He fiddled with his inkwell. He stared at the ceiling. He toyed with his mustache.

Quietly, he ordered, "Count the money."

George and Richard looked at each other. Gingerly, George reached for the small sack. He felt as if he was putting his hand in hot coals as he slowly pulled out the money. He did not look at Mr. Koller, but directly at the money as he counted every cent into Richard's trembling hands, occasionally pausing for Richard to stack the money on the headmaster's desk. When he was through he glanced up at Mr. Koller, who seemed to be deep in thought.

The tension was unbearable. But if he was taking so long to make a decision, George reasoned, that had to be a good sign, didn't it? Perhaps he was trying to decide what punishment would be appropriate. *I'll do anything,* George thought, *if he'll just give me another chance.*

At last Mr. Koller stood. He looked at each boy with a mixture of regret and resignation.

"I'm sorry, gentlemen, but you simply leave me no choice. The Bristol Academy is known for upholding not only the highest academic standards, but the highest moral standards. And I'm afraid you two do not meet our requirements. Effective immediately, you are both expelled."

❧ Seventeen ❧

Y ou're pacing again."

Christy smiled at the headmaster's secretary, Miss Murkoff. "I'm sorry. I can't seem to stop myself."

It seemed as if she'd been waiting here for hours, but in truth, it had only been a short while. Behind the closed door that led to Mr. Koller's office, Christy heard a deep, rumbling male voice.

Once again she tried to imagine how things were going on the other side of that door. Were Richard and George going to be able to stay here at the academy? Christy had been so sure that urging George to tell the truth would solve matters. But now, as the minutes ticked by, she was almost beginning to have some doubts.

"Would you like some more tea?" asked Miss Murkoff, a slender woman whose white hair was pulled back in a tidy bun.

"Oh, no, I'm fine. You've been so kind already, keeping me company." While Christy waited, Miss Murkoff had entertained her with stories about the academy, the staff, and the many students she'd seen come and go over the years.

Miss Murkoff glanced at the headmaster's door. "I do hope everything works out for George. He's such a fine boy. I've always had a soft spot in my heart for him. On my birthday, he brought me a bouquet of paper flowers."

"He does love to do his magic tricks," Christy said.

Mr. Koller's voice rose, muffled behind the heavy door. Christy bit her lip anxiously.

"Don't worry," Miss Murkoff said. "Mr. Koller's bark is worse than his bite." She paused. "Usually, anyway. He can be stern when he has to be."

"I remember George telling me once that all the boys are afraid of him."

"Well, I suppose that's true. He doesn't tolerate misbehavior, and he expects our students to follow the rules. But he has to be that way, in order to keep things from getting out of control. You can imagine how rowdy boys this age can be."

Christy managed a smile, recalling some of George's antics over the years. "Yes, I suppose it's hard to keep order."

"Still, he's a fine man, Mr. Koller. I'm sure he'll be fair with your brother."

"I guess that's all I can ask for."

"I've worked here for many, many years," Miss Murkoff said. "And I've come to respect Mr. Koller tremendously."

Again Mr. Koller's voice rose. It was hard for Christy to catch any words, but the tone was unmistakably angry.

Miss Murkoff gave a small, wry smile, "Yes, I respect him tremendously. Even if he *can* be a bit gruff sometimes."

Just then, the door slowly opened. George and Richard emerged.

"Well?" Christy asked, but she could tell from their expressions what the answer was.

She threw her arms around George. "I'm so sorry," she whispered.

George shrugged. "Mr. Koller's right. We deserve to be punished for what happened. I only wish Richard could have stayed. . . ."

"It's my fault this whole thing happened," Richard said. "I don't deserve to stay."

As they departed, Miss Murkoff gave a small wave. "Goodbye, boys. I'll miss you." She clucked her tongue softly. "I really did love those magic flowers."

~ ~ ~

They walked slowly to the dormitory and collected their belongings. As they headed down the long walk to the front gate of the academy, no one spoke.

At last Richard said, "You were right about one thing, Miss Huddleston. I do feel better. I told the truth and returned the money, and that was the right thing to do. But now, I've ruined George's life. And my sister's right back where she started . . ."

The guard opened the gate and they exited.

"My life isn't ruined, pal," George said, slapping Richard on the back. "Why, who knows what adventures await me, now that I'm free from the confines of the Bristol Academy? It always *was* a stodgy old school. From here on out, I intend to learn my lessons in the school of life."

But despite his optimistic manner, George couldn't disguise his fear. Christy patted her brother on the shoulder. "I really thought it would turn out differently. Did you explain the whole story to Mr. Koller?"

"As much as we could," George said, "but Mr. Koller did most of the talking."

Behind them, an automobile approached. Its horn gave a loud honk. Christy spun around to see a familiar sight. "It's Father," she cried, "and Mother, too!"

The car came to a stop behind them and Mr. and Mrs. Huddleston leapt out. They each took turns warmly embracing Christy and

George. Mrs. Huddleston even gave Richard an extra-long hug.

"You shouldn't have come," George said uncomfortably.

"We wanted to, son," Mr. Huddleston replied.

Mrs. Huddleston cleared her throat, and Mr. Huddleston added, "Well, if the truth be told, we were angry at first—and disappointed. But the more we thought about the way your sister was supporting you . . . we knew we had to follow her example."

"Have you spoken to Mr. Koller yet?" Mrs. Huddleston asked.

"We were expelled," George muttered, head hung low.

"Oh my," Mrs. Huddleston said.

"Please don't blame George for any of this," Richard interjected. "It's really all my fault."

"We know the whole story, Richard," Mr. Huddleston assured him. "I'm just sorry it had to end this way."

"Maybe . . . " Christy paused, glancing back at the sprawling academy buildings, "maybe it doesn't have to end this way."

"What do you mean, Sis?" George asked.

"I'm going back to the headmaster's," Christy said firmly.

"Christy, dear," said Mrs. Huddleston, "if your brother couldn't convince Mr. Koller to give him a second chance, then I hardly think you'll have better luck."

"George may be charming, Mother," Christy said, winking at her brother, "but I've learned a thing or two about people in the past year. Wait for me here. I won't be long."

❧ Eighteen ❧

W hy, Miss Huddleston," Miss Murkoff exclaimed when Christy returned, "did you forget something?"

"Actually, I did," Christy said breathlessly. "I forgot to request a brief meeting with Mr. Koller."

"It's getting late, and he's got another appointment in five minutes." Miss Murkoff consulted her calendar and clucked her tongue. "Peter Smithers—a real discipline problem."

"I promise it will only take a minute or two."

"Let me see if Mr. Koller will meet with you. Generally, after expelling a student . . . well, you understand. He prefers not to meet with the family." Miss Murkoff smiled at Christy. "But I'll tell him what a nice chat you and I had, and maybe I can convince him to see you."

Miss Murkoff knocked on the headmaster's door and slipped inside. A few moments later, she emerged. "He'll see you," she said, "but just for a minute."

As Christy stepped into Mr. Koller's office, she could imagine the fear her brother and Richard must have felt. Mr. Koller was an impressive figure—even more so when he greeted her in his booming voice.

"To begin with, Miss Huddleston, I'm afraid I must tell you, that in my many years as headmaster, I have never changed my mind about an expulsion," he began, gesturing her toward a leather chair. "I don't make such decisions lightly, I can assure you. And the gravity of the offense committed by your brother and his roommate cannot be overlooked."

"I understand," Christy said. Her voice sounded tinny and small after Mr. Koller's words. "And I was as upset and disappointed by what they did as anyone. I firmly believe they should be punished, too."

"Then you came here to tell me we're in agreement?" Mr. Koller pulled at his mustache. "I must say that's unusual behavior for a family member."

"Well, we're in agreement, but not entirely," Christy said. "Mr. Koller, did Richard or George tell you *why* the money was stolen?"

Mr. Koller shook his head. "No."

"Richard's family has been having money problems," Christy said. "His sister broke her leg a few months ago, and there was no money to have it properly cared for. The leg set badly, and the girl is in constant pain. Now the only hope is for her to have expensive surgery."

Mr. Koller swiveled his chair and looked out the window behind his desk. "I'm sorry to hear that."

"That's the reason Richard took the money, Mr. Koller," Christy continued. "I know it doesn't in any way excuse his behavior, and Richard knows it, too. That's why he came back here. To return the money and set things right—even though he believed that money may well have been his sister's only hope."

Mr. Koller turned back to Christy. "As sympathetic as I am to Richard's plight, I cannot excuse such behavior. He's lucky I didn't turn him in to the authorities."

"I'm not asking you to excuse his behavior." Christy went to the edge of Mr. Koller's desk, her voice pleading. "All I'm saying is the punishment should fit the crime. This is Richard's one chance at obtaining an education—and quite possibly, George's. Haven't other boys at Bristol been punished in other ways?"

"Most certainly. With detentions or with work assignments on the grounds. But those aren't boys who stole money from under my very nose and then lied about it. I'm sorry, Miss Huddleston, but any leniency is strictly out of the question."

"Mr. Koller," Christy said so quietly that the headmaster had to lean forward to hear her, "sometimes students do things that embarrass their teachers. I know it must be distressing to have a student do this, as you said, 'right under your nose.'"

"Yes," he admitted. "And, I know where you are headed with this conversation, but I would not let embarrassment influence my decision," he said indignantly.

"I guess there's nothing I can say to change your mind?"

"If I listened to every pleading family member who came through this door, discipline at Bristol would be impossible. Now, if you'll excuse me, I have business to attend to." Mr. Koller gave a slight smile. "I must say, however, that I admire your sisterly loyalty."

Christy's gaze fell on a family photograph on the corner of Mr. Koller's desk. "Is that your sister, by any chance?"

"Why . . . why, yes." Mr. Koller gazed fondly at the sepia-toned photo. "But how did you guess—?"

"Miss Murkoff told me a lot about you while I was waiting."

"Yes, she can be quite the talker."

"She mentioned that your sister was paralyzed in an accident when she was four."

Mr. Koller nodded. "It was a hard time," he said softly.

"What if, as a young man, you'd thought there was a way you could have helped her walk again?" Christy asked.

Mr. Koller stared at the photograph as if he were traveling through time. "I suppose," he said, "if I'd thought I could do something to help her, I would have done it, no matter what."

The admission seemed to surprise him. He sat very still, eyes closed. The only sound in the room was the ticking of his grandfather clock.

At last he opened his eyes and turned to Christy. A smile slowly formed on his face. "My, my, but you are a persuasive young woman. May I ask what you do for a living?"

"I'm the teacher at a mission school in Tennessee."

Mr. Koller took a deep breath and stood. "I'm going to give your brother and his friend a second chance, Miss Huddleston. They will do so much work around here and suffer through so many detentions that they may wish I hadn't let them come back. But if they persevere and don't stray again, I may just see you again someday . . . at their graduation ceremony. Thanks, in large measure, to one very loyal and loving sister."

Christy smiled at the headmaster. "You are a fair man, Mr. Koller," she said.

"I try," he replied. Then after a pause, he gently said, "Would you tell me more about Richard's family?"

❦ Nineteen ❧

W ell?" George asked.

"How'd it go?" Richard questioned softly.

The two boys and Christy's parents were leaning against the parked automobile, waiting expectantly.

Christy cleared her throat, her face grave. "I'm sure you realize what a stern man Mr. Koller is," she began.

"He's tough," Richard agreed.

"The toughest," said George.

"And I'm sure you both realize the gravity of your crimes."

Both boys nodded.

"So you didn't have any luck?" George asked in a resigned voice.

"Well, I didn't say that." Christy broke into a grin. "Let's just say you're going to be facing lots of punishment. But you're staying in school. Both of you."

"Christy!" George lifted her into his arms and whirled her around till she was dizzy. "You're amazing! You are the most amazing, incredible, wonderful sister—"

"George, please put me down before I get sick," Christy instructed.

Richard gave her an awkward hug. "I don't know how to thank you," he said.

"I'll tell you how you can both thank me," Christy said as she straightened her dress. "Do not get into any more trouble between now and graduation. Understand?"

George saluted her. "You have my word."

"And mine," Richard added softly.

"Richard," Mrs. Huddleston said. "You don't seem all that happy, dear."

"Oh, I am. I'm really grateful to Christy for getting me a second chance. It's just that I was thinking about Abigail, my little sister. I feel sort of guilty about the idea of continuing school. Maybe if I got a job instead . . ."

"Give it some time, Richard," Christy advised. "Doctor MacNeill said he was going to get in touch with some of his friends. Maybe something will work out."

"And we could talk to some people from our church about putting together a fund for Abigail," Mr. Huddleston offered.

"Don't give up yet, Richard," George advised. "By now, it should be pretty obvious that my sister is capable of magical feats."

"Turns out you're not the only magician in the family," Christy said with a wink.

* * *

Five weeks later, Mr. Pentland brought Christy a letter one afternoon just as school was about to let out for the day. She read the return address and gasped.

"It's from George!" she exclaimed. "I can't believe it. He hardly *ever* writes letters!"

While the children gathered around, she tore open the envelope excitedly. This was one letter she definitely couldn't wait to read.

Christy was surprised to find two letters in the envelope—one from George and one from Richard. Slowly, she began to read George's out loud:

> Dear Christy,
>
> Surprise! Bet you never thought you'd see a letter from yours truly. But I wanted to write and say thank you, once again, for everything you did for Richard and me.
>
> Mr. Koller's assigned us to every work detail you can imagine—caring for the grounds, washing blackboards, even helping in the dining room. (Tell Doc MacNeill my cooking skills have definitely improved.)

But we're grateful for the punishment. We know it means a second chance at school, and we're not going to make any mistakes this time.

We've got a few days off next month, and Mr. Koller's even letting Richard and me leave the school grounds. Richard's going home to visit his family. But, I'll let him tell you his news in his own letter.

I thought I might head back to Cutter Gap for another visit—that is, if you'll have me. I promise not to disrupt class or otherwise misbehave.

Your loving brother,
George

P.S. I really will try to write more often.

"George is a-comin!" Creed cried. "George is a-comin' back!"

The children laughed and applauded, and Christy was proud to realize she didn't feel the least bit jealous. In fact, she felt like laughing and applauding herself.

Only Ruby Mae seemed a bit skeptical. "I'll believe it when I see it," she said, arms crossed over her chest. "That George is a most unreliable boy, if'n you ask me."

"Read the other letter, Miz Christy," someone urged.

Christy turned to Richard's letter and read:

Dear Miss Huddleston,

I am writing on behalf of my family to thank you, Doctor MacNeill, the people at the mission, and your parents' congregation for your help.

Thanks to your generosity, and the generosity of Doctor MacNeill's fellow physicians, Abigail is now recovering from her surgery of last week. She is in some pain, but the doctors tell us they expect a complete recovery. And Abigail is confident she'll be up and around by her birthday next month.

And thanks to a contact of your father's, my father has begun a new job at the railroad office in town. It has been a long time since I have seen him so happy, or so full of hope. And it's all thanks to this miracle you helped bring about.

It has been a long time since I have felt so hopeful, too.

Thank you again for all you have done.

Yours truly,
Richard Benton

Christy tucked the letter back into its envelope. "Don't thank me, Richard," she whispered. "Thank God. He's the miracle worker."

❧ Twenty ❧

I just cannot wait to see that charming young man again," Miss Ida said excitedly as she bustled about the mission kitchen a few weeks later. "I do hope he gets here soon. I have such a feast planned."

"So you've forgiven George for everything?" Christy asked.

Miss Ida grinned. "Well, I was a little miffed about the way he lied to us. But now that the whole story's out, and he's being properly punished at school . . . well, it seems like it's time to forgive and forget."

"He is a little late," Christy said, glancing out the window. "It's nearly dark, and he should have made it here by now. Maybe I should have gone to meet him at the train station."

"He'll be here," said Doctor MacNeill. "Don't you worry. He wouldn't dare miss Miss Ida's cooking."

"Speaking of missing persons," said Miss Alice as she finished setting the table, "has anyone seen Ruby Mae?"

"Not for an hour or two," Christy replied. "Maybe she's feeding Prince."

"Or maybe," a voice called from the parlor, "she's assisting George the Magnificent in his amazing magical extravaganza!"

"That sounded like . . ." Christy began.

She ran into the parlor. There stood George, dressed in his best suit and wearing a tall, black top hat. Next to him stood Ruby Mae, wearing a sparkling bead turban and pink feather cape.

"Ladies and gentlemen," said George in his smoothest magician voice, "allow me to introduce my incredible assistant, Ruby Mae the Remarkable!"

Ruby Mae took a low bow.

"But how long have you been here?" Christy cried, rushing over to give her brother a big hug.

"Long enough to prepare a wonderful magic show for your entertainment," George replied with a wink. "We've been practicing over at the schoolhouse. My assistant and I are prepared to delight and amaze you."

"How about if you delight and amaze us *after* dinner?" Miss Alice suggested. "Miss Ida's put together a wonderful meal in your honor, George."

"How about it, Ruby Mae?" George asked.

"Sounds good to me. My stomach's a-rumblin' somethin' fierce," Ruby Mae replied. "Magic is hard work." She headed for the dining room. "Well, come on, everybody. Let's dig in!"

As everyone gathered around the table, Ruby Mae tugged on Christy's arm. "Told ya he'd be back," she said. She cast George a flirtatious smile. "You're so lucky to have a brother like him. I just wish he could stay forever. Don't you, Miz Christy?"

Christy glanced across the table. George was in the middle of telling a joke. As usual, all eyes were on her brother.

He would always be charming. He would always be the center of attention. And he would always be a little unpredictable.

And she would always love him.

"You know, Ruby Mae," Christy said, "I wish he could stay forever, too."

About the Author

Catherine Marshall

With *Christy*, Catherine Marshall LeSourd (1914–1983) created one of the world's most widely read and best-loved classics. Published in 1967, the book spent 39 weeks on the New York Times bestseller list. With an estimated 30 million Americans having read it, *Christy* is now approaching its 90th printing and has sold more than eight million copies. Although a novel, *Christy* is in fact a thinly-veiled biography of Catherine's mother, Leonora Wood.

Catherine Marshall LeSourd also authored *A Man Called Peter*, which has sold more than four million copies. It is an American bestseller, portraying the love between a dynamic man and his God, and the tender, romantic love between a man and the girl he married.

Another one of Catherine's books is *Julie*, a powerful, sweeping novel of love and adventure, courage and commitment, tragedy and triumph, in a Pennsylvania town during the Great Depression. Catherine also authored many other devotional books of encouragement.

THE CHRISTY® FICTION SERIES

You'll want to read them all!

Based upon Catherine Marshall's international bestseller *Christy*®, this new series contains expanded adventures filled with romance, intrigue, and excitement.

#1—The Bridge to Cutter Gap
Nineteen-year-old Christy leaves her family to teach at a mission school in the Great Smoky Mountains. On the other side of an icy bridge lie excitement, adventure, and maybe even the man of her dreams . . . but can she survive a life-and-death struggle when she falls into the rushing waters below? (ISBN 0-8499-3686-1)

#2—Silent Superstitions
Christy's students are suddenly afraid to come to school. Is what Granny O'Teale says true? Is their teacher cursed? Will the children's fears and the adults' superstitions force Christy to abandon her dreams and return to North Carolina? (ISBN 0-8499-3687-X)

#3—The Angry Intruder
Someone wants Christy to leave Cutter Gap, and they'll stop at nothing. Mysterious pranks soon turn dangerous. Could a student be the culprit? When Christy confronts the late-night intruder, will it be a face she knows? (ISBN 0-8499-3688-8)

#4—Midnight Rescue
The mission's black stallion, Prince, has vanished, and so has Christy's student Ruby Mae. Christy must brave the guns of angry moonshiners to bring them home. Will her faith in God see her through her darkest night? (ISBN 0-8499-3689-6)

#5—The Proposal
Christy should be thrilled when David Grantland, the handsome minister, proposes marriage, but her feelings of excitement are mixed with confusion and uncertainty. Several untimely interruptions delay her answer to David's proposal. Then a terrible riding accident and blindness threaten all of Christy's dreams for the future. (ISBN 0-8499-3918-6)

#6—Christy's Choice
When Christy is offered a chance to teach in her hometown, she faces a difficult decision. Will her train ride back to Cutter Gap be a journey home or a last farewell? In a moment of terror and danger, Christy must decide where her future lies. (ISBN 0-8499-3919-4)

#7—The Princess Club
When Ruby Mae, Bessie, and Clara discover gold at Cutter Gap, they form an exclusive organization, "The Princess Club." Christy watches in dismay as her classroom—and her community—are torn apart by greed, envy, and an understanding of what true wealth really means. (ISBN 0-8499-3958-5)

#8—Family Secrets
Bob Allen and many of the residents of Cutter Gap are upset when a black family, the Washingtons, moves in near the Allens' property. When a series of threatening incidents befall the Washingtons, Christy steps in to help. But it's a clue in the Washingtons' family Bible that may hold the real key to peace and acceptance. (ISBN 0-8499-3959-3)

#9—Mountain Madness
When Christy travels alone to a nearby mountain, she vows to discover the truth behind the terrifying

legend of a strange mountain creature. But what she finds, at first seems worse than she ever imagined! (ISBN 0-8499-3960-7)

#10—Stage Fright
As Christy's students are preparing for a school play, she reveals her dream to act on stage herself. Little does she know that Doctor MacNeill's aunt is the artistic director of the Knoxville theater. Before long, just as Christy is about to debut on stage, several mysterious incidents threaten both her dreams and her pride! (ISBN 0-8499-3961-5)

#11—Goodbye, Sweet Prince
Prince, the mission's stallion, is sold to a cruel owner, then disappears. Christy Huddleston and her students are heartsick. Is there any way to reclaim the magnificent horse? (ISBN 0-8499-3962-3)

#12—Brotherly Love
Everyone is delighted when Christy's younger brother, George Huddleston, visits Christy at the Cutter Gap Mission. But the delight ends when George reveals that he has been expelled from school for stealing. Can Christy summon the love and faith to help her brother do the right thing? (ISBN 0-8499-3963-1)

Christy is now available on home videos through Broadman & Holman Publishers.